DeKok and

the Mask of Death

Inspector DeKok Investigates

Speck Press is proud to present Dutch author Albert Cornelis Baantjer's Inspector DeKok Investigates series in English. This highly acclaimed series provides a snapshot into the career of the fictional detective, his young partner, and the historic Warmoes Street Station in Amsterdam.

More than fifty novels were published in the Netherlands, beginning in the mid-sixties, with releases over the following decades.

Other Available Titles

DeKok and
the Mask of Death

by

Baantjer

Translated by H. G. Smittenaar

speck press
golden

Published by Speck Press
An imprint of Fulcrum Publishing
4690 Table Mountain Drive, Suite 100 • Golden, Colorado 80403
800-992-2908 • 303-277-1623 • speckpress.com

ISBN: 978-1-933108-30-8

Library of Congress Cataloging-in-Publication Data

Baantjer, A. C.
[De Cock en het masker van de dood]
DeKok and the mask of death / by A.C. Baantjer ; translated from the
Dutch by H.G. Smittenaar.
    p. cm. -- (Inspector Dekok series ; no. 25)
ISBN 978-1-933108-30-8
I. Smittenaar, H. G. II. Title.
PT5881.12.A2D57513 2009
839.31'364--dc22
                                  2009011425
10 9 8 7 6 5 4 3 2 1

Book layout and design by Margaret McCullough
Cover image © Shutterstock
Printed in the United States of America by Malloy Inc.

1

Inspector DeKok, of Amsterdam's venerable police station on Warmoes Street, ambled leisurely over the wide pavement of the Damrak. Every once in a while he would squint at the generous sun that, despite the dire forecasts of a depression over the North Sea, refused to hide behind the gray clouds. For days it had been shining brightly in a clear, blue sky.

DeKok enjoyed himself. His attitude had the characteristics of a human barometer: when it was cold and rainy his face looked stormy, but it brightened immediately with the slightest indication of warmer weather. A smile would form, his heart rejoiced, and his old, dilapidated hat would tilt carelessly to one side of his gray-haired head.

He stopped on the corner of Old Bridge Alley. For just a moment he entertained the thought of leaving crime fighting behind and continuing his walk in the bright sunshine, out of the narrow streets of the quarter, toward the Amstel River, and along its banks to the green meadows, where peaceful cows grazed among white, innocent sheep.

He grinned ruefully at himself and hastily crossed the Damrak to the other side, completely ignoring an approaching streetcar. Then he relaxed his pace and strolled past the Skipper's Exchange until he turned onto Warmoes Street.

Standing in front of the station house, DeKok contemplated the worn bluestone steps hollowed out over the years by the footsteps of cops and sinners. The steps felt like a barrier, a barrier that filled him with an unreasonable fear that cooled the bright sunlight and sent a shivering chill of dread through his bones. It was as if a strange inner voice whispered to him, urging him to forego his life for a day and take a leap into the future. Shrugging off the inexplicable fear, DeKok climbed the steps and pushed open the door.

When he reached the large detective room on the second floor, Vledder—his partner, friend, and apprentice—looked at him searchingly.

"What's the matter? You look frightened."

"What do you mean?"

"You look pale, as if you've seen a ghost."

DeKok threw his hat in the direction of the peg. As usual, he missed but did not bother to retrieve it from the floor. He pulled off his raincoat and folded it over the back of his chair.

"Do you believe in omens?"

"Good omens or bad omens?" mocked Vledder.

DeKok shook his head in disapproval.

"You shouldn't dismiss them," he said earnestly. "Omens are unfathomable portents, harbingers of things to come...usually something bad, or shocking." He stared off into the distance. "A few minutes ago, I experienced an omen, a premonition," he continued. "I was standing in front of the station house and was suddenly overwhelmed with the feeling that I should not enter the building. It was as if the bluestone steps spoke to me about a warning of an approaching disaster."

Vledder grinned.

"Nonsense. Stones don't speak." He tilted his head to one side. "I think you have a slight summer flu. It's going around at the moment. And you know, feverish people have the strangest hallucinations sometimes."

"I don't have the flu and I'm not feverish," DeKok responded brusquely. "You may forget my omen, if you like." He felt the chill in his bones. "But you're the one who asked why I was so pale when I came in."

Vledder smiled.

"An omen."

"Exactly."

Vledder leaned closer.

"Early this morning, the commissaris stopped by and asked for you."

"Why?"

"He wants to speak with you."

"What about?"

Vledder waved vaguely.

"There's a rumor going around that you will be put in charge of a special antipickpocket detail."

DeKok looked disgusted.

"Me...an antipickpocket detail?"

Vledder nodded.

"Next week starts Operation Sail Amsterdam. Large crowds are expected to attend to see the sailing ships enter the port. And, of course, they'll hang around visiting the ships and so on. All the hotels are already booked to capacity. It's an ideal event for the international pickpocket guild. And it will give *you* the opportunity to look at some old scows."

DeKok looked up, irritation on his weathered face.

"What's the matter with you? Didn't you sleep well? Why are you so negative? First you mock my omen and now you degrade the glory of centuries of shipping to...to a bunch of old scows."

Vledder looked innocent.

"Aren't they old scows?"

DeKok closed his eyes and sighed deeply.

"Sail Amsterdam is a wonderful display. As an ex-Urker, I'm very attached to those old sailing ships. My grandfather fished with his graceful smack on what was still the Zuyder Zee. No noisy engines of hundreds of horsepower, just sails. Trusting in God and the wind. I'm determined to spend a lot of time studying the spectacle on the Ij. I missed the last Sail Amsterdam altogether because we were tangled up with that case on the inheritance of that psychiatrist. But this time I will not miss it. So the commissaris can find someone else for his antipickpocket detail."

"You're taking leave?"

DeKok nodded emphatically.

"Exactly. I certainly have enough leave on the books. I'm going to enjoy myself. I'm going to see the *Amerigo Vespucci* from Italy, the *Kruzenshtern* from Germany, the *Libertad* from Argentina, the *Danish Georg Stage*, and the *American Eagle*...you know, it's still a Coast Guard cutter on active service." A melancholy smile curled his lips.

"Magnificent examples of shipbuilding as it used to be. Graceful beauties, every last one of them…living memories of a time gone by: the time of romance, exploration, heroic feats of seamanship, shanties."

Vledder looked lost.

"What exactly are shanties?"

DeKok spread both arms wide in an expression of delight.

"Seafaring songs! During their heavy and sometimes monotonous work aboard the windjammers, seamen sang their shanties, like 'Rolling Home' and 'What Shall We Do with a Drunken Sailor?'"

Vledder listened to the enthusiastic tone.

"You were born too late," Vledder replied.

DeKok laughed in agreement.

There was a sudden knock on the door. The detective nearest the door called out, "Enter."

The door opened slowly. A young man stood in the doorway. The man turned to the detective nearest the door and asked a question. The detective pointed at Vledder and DeKok. The young man nodded his thanks and turned to approach the two desks in the back of the room.

DeKok estimated the visitor to be in his late twenties. He was rather tall and spare. His pale face had a receding chin. He wore a dark brown tweed jacket with leather patches on the elbows and light gray creaseless trousers. The sleeves of the jacket were too short for his long arms. He approached hesitantly with a shy smile. A few feet from DeKok's desk he stopped and looked from DeKok to Vledder and back again.

"She's gone," he said. There was an apologetic, confused tone to his voice.

"She's gone," he repeated in the same tone of voice.

DeKok eyed him carefully. He looked at the friendly gray eyes, the low forehead, and the disorderly, heavy mop of brown hair. The young man looked so clumsy and inept that the old inspector was touched. He beckoned him closer and asked him to sit in the chair next to his desk.

"Who's gone?" he asked winningly.

"Rosie."

"Rosie?" repeated DeKok.

The young man nodded.

"That's what I call her. Rosie. Actually her name is Rosalind, Rosalind Evertsoord. She's nobility." He gestured timidly. "Impoverished nobility."

"And who are you?"

The young man bolted upright. He made a stiff bow.

"I'm sorry," he said, contrite. "That was inexcusable. I should have introduced myself at once. My name is Richard Netherwood." He resumed his seat. "And you are Inspector DeKok."

"With a kay-oh-kay," added DeKok.

Richard smiled.

"I was told you would say that."

DeKok gave him a questioning look.

"Who told you that?"

"Friends of mine. They advised that I should contact you."

"In connection with Rosie?"

"Yes. I first went to the police station in Slotermeer. But they wouldn't listen to me. Not really, I mean."

"But Slotermeer is all the way in Amsterdam-West. Why would you go there?"

Richard Netherwood seemed unsure of himself.

"That…that's where the case was to be handled."

"Why?"

"It happened in Slotervaart Hospital, and that area is covered by the police station in Slotermeer."

DeKok rubbed his face with a flat hand.

"Very well, what happened at Slotervaart Hospital?"

"That's where Rosie disappeared."

"Just like that?"

The young man moved in his chair.

"You're right," he said, shaking his head. "I'm starting this a bit chaotically. You must excuse me. I'm a bit upset, confused by all this. I will try to be more coherent."

DeKok gave him an encouraging nod.

"What is your relationship with Rosie?"

"She's my girlfriend. We've had a relationship for years. I live on Church Street, close to the Amstel. Rosie lives outside the city in Purmerend. We usually get together on weekends. And we always take our vacations together."

Richard reached into an inside pocket, produced a photograph, and handed it to DeKok.

"This is her."

The gray sleuth looked at the laughing face of a young woman with short, blond hair. Her smile and the dimples in her cheeks gave the face a pleasant aura. DeKok wondered what such a pretty girl saw in this tall, gawky young man. But he wisely kept the thought to himself. He took another look at the picture and was just about to return it when Richard put his hand up.

"You keep it. For your investigation. You'll probably need it."

DeKok handed the picture to Vledder, who placed it on his desk.

"How did Rosie wind up in Slotervaart Hospital?"

"She was referred by her house doctor, Dr. Aken, in Purmerend."

"Was she ill?"

Richard shrugged.

"Rosie is never sick. She's very athletic. Plays a lot of basketball, she's very good. She plays with teams that represent our country. But the last few days she felt a bit under the weather. She was lethargic, listless. She coughed a little. That's what she told me over the phone. We call each other every day. At my urging, she went to see her doctor."

DeKok gave him a puzzled look.

"And the doctor referred her to the hospital here in Amsterdam?"

"Yes."

"Why not a hospital in Purmerend?"

The young man shrugged again.

"I don't know. Frankly, I never thought about it."

"To which department was she referred?"

"Neurology."

DeKok gestured.

"And what else?"

Richard Netherwood did not answer at once. He stared into the distance for several seconds. It was as if he was trying to visualize the hospital.

"Rosie," he said hoarsely, "reported with her referral to the desk."

"When was that?"

"Day before yesterday, Wednesday, eleven o'clock in the morning."

"You were with her?"

Richard nodded.

"She wanted me to come with her. She drove her own car from Purmerend to Amsterdam. A Citroën 'Ugly Duckling,' garishly painted. She honked her horn in front of my house and I got in. From there we drove to the hospital. We were both a bit depressed."

DeKok again smiled encouragingly.

"I can understand that. Please go on."

Netherwood licked dry lips.

"There is a big parking lot next to the hospital. That's where she parked. We stepped out of the car and looked up. I immediately had a bad feeling about the building. It was so big, so cold and sterile, so impersonal that it scared me. I even thought about stopping Rosie from going in. But I realized how idiotic my fear really was."

DeKok's face became serious.

"Although the immediate reason may be nebulous, fear is never idiotic."

Richard gave him a grateful look.

"Yes, I felt the fear. It was very real. I was literally shaking in my boots. The entire distance to the entrance I clamped Rosie's arm under mine. I was afraid to lose her." He sighed deeply. "Inside, I had to let her go. She walked by herself to the front desk. Somebody told her to wait a moment."

"A moment?"

"A few minutes, I think. Then a nurse came. She called out Rosie's name and took her away."

"And you remained in the lobby?"

Richard made an apologetic gesture.

"I didn't think it would take long, fifteen minutes or half an hour at most. But after an hour, I was still waiting." He grinned, embarrassed. "I'm not the kind of person who immediately makes a nuisance of himself. It's just not in me. So I calmly kept waiting. But for some unknown reason, I became more and more worried. Finally, I couldn't force myself to sit in that chair any longer. I left the lobby and started to pace the corridor. I had just gathered enough courage to ask some questions when the same nurse came up to me and asked me to follow her. I thought she would take me to Rosie or to a doctor, a specialist who would tell me about her condition...if there was anything wrong. But she took me to some kind of consultation room, where another nurse took some of my blood."

DeKok looked at his visitor in disbelief.

"What?" he asked. "They took some of your blood?"

Richard nodded.

"And you allowed that?"

Richard shrugged with one shoulder.

"I, eh, I thought," he said reluctantly, "that it had something to do with Rosie's medical examination. That they wanted to know if I had something...a disease, or something like that."

DeKok took a deep breath.

"You allowed a blood sample to be taken." It sounded like an accusation.

Richard nodded.

"When it was done, the nurse who had picked me up in the corridor said that that was all and I could leave. I told her that I wasn't leaving yet. That I was waiting for Ms. Evertsoord. She looked at me as if surprised, a bit absentmindedly, and said, 'Miss Evertsoord?' and I said, 'Yes, that's the lady you came to get from the lobby about an hour ago.' She looked me straight in the face, shook her head, and denied she had picked up any woman in the lobby."

"And that was the same nurse?"

"Absolutely."

DeKok smiled and leaned closer.

"You were out of your normal routine," he said in a friendly, calming tone of voice. "Because of the long wait you were a bit stressed. I can imagine —"

Richard interrupted him abruptly.

"There's no mistake," he said, loud and determined. "That face, the somewhat plump figure of the nurse, I'll never forget that." He pointed at his forehead. "It's etched in my brain." Red spots appeared on his cheeks and he snorted contemptuously. "She just walked away from me."

"Who?"

Richard gesticulated agitatedly.

"That nurse! She walked down the corridor. I followed her and took her by the arm. 'Where is Rosie?' I screamed at her. 'What have you done with her!?' The nurse became angry. She pushed my hand from her arm and she said in that snotty voice that I shouldn't bother her. Then she went through a door and was gone. I was stunned. I felt as if somebody had just hit me on the head with a baseball bat."

He paused to take a deep breath.

"When I had myself more or less under control," he continued, "I went back to the lobby and walked over to the man behind the desk. As politely as possible I told him that I had arrived with Rosie that morning. He asked me her name and I gave it to him. 'She had a referral from Dr. Aken, in Purmerend,' I said."

"Was it the same man who was there when Rosie checked in?"

"Yes. He looked at some papers and said that she wasn't on his list and if she wasn't on his list, she could not have checked in with him."

Richard clapped his hands over his eyes. His body shook. Sweat beaded on his forehead. It took a while before he could continue. DeKok waited patiently.

"For a moment I thought I'd gone crazy," said Richard. "I stood there a long time in front of the desk. The man ignored me, acted as if I wasn't there. Numbed into a sort of dull panic, I left the hospital. It felt as if my brain was rattling around in my skull. Outside, I suddenly remembered Rosie's car. As fast as I could, I ran across the parking lot."

DeKok looked at him.

"And?" he asked tensely.

Richard's head sank to his chest.

"Her car was gone."

2

After Richard Netherwood left the detective room, a deep silence fell. It was one of those rare moments when all noise suddenly stops. Vledder and DeKok looked at each other. One detective put down a telephone receiver and another rested his fingers on a keyboard and stared in thought at his screen. Even the street noise paused. For several seconds, in that strange silence, it was as if the tale of the young man still clung to the walls. Then a telephone rang and the weird lull evaporated as quickly as it had begun.

Vledder shook his head as if to clear it. He looked at DeKok with a skeptical smile.

"Do you believe that strange story?"

DeKok answered with a question.

"Do you believe it?"

Vledder made an indecisive gesture.

"It is, eh, an absurd tale. As far as I'm concerned, his girlfriend, if she was his girlfriend, simply ran away. And when you take a look at that guy, I can't blame her much."

"I must confess that for a moment I wondered what such a pretty girl saw in such a gawky young man. But they have had a relationship for years. I'm sure we see men in a different way than women do."

"Maybe. But I still think she wanted to be rid of him."

DeKok pursed his lips.

"A very unusual and uncivil way to break off a relationship," he said with disapproval in his voice.

Vledder laughed.

"I can see the humor in it. Young people these days are no longer as formal as in the past. She just let him sit there in the lobby, like a fool. And then she took off in her own car. It seems clear to me. A definite rejection."

DeKok shook his head.

"And what about the nurse?" he asked carefully. "Richard said she denied flatly that she had escorted Rosie from the lobby."

Vledder shrugged.

"Perhaps Ms. Evertsoord took the nurse into her confidence, told her what she planned to do, and the nurse played along."

"And the man behind the desk?"

Vledder spread both arms.

"The same thing." He gestured at the door through which Richard had disappeared. "That type just asks for it."

DeKok looked puzzled.

"Asks for what?"

"To be fooled."

"So you consider him to be some kind of village idiot?"

Vledder waved nonchalantly.

"No, I don't want to go that far," he said, irritated. "But it is a fact that there are young men who are just not taken seriously by women. The girls snicker at them."

"And Richard Netherwood is that type?"

"I think so." He reached for the photograph and looked at it. "A nice, pretty, athletic girl." He snorted. "If you ask me, there is no question of any relationship. That guy just imagines it."

"So, a village idiot after all?"

Vledder threw the photo on his desk.

"I don't know about you, but I wouldn't give a wooden nickel for his story."

DeKok ignored the remark. He sat up in his chair and stretched out a hand toward his young friend.

"Why don't you call Slotermeer Station and ask if they have done anything with the case, just to be sure. Although I suspect that the answer will be no. If that is the case, get in contact with the chief administrator or the head doctor of Slotervaart Hospital and ask him if it will be convenient to receive us this afternoon for an interview. Also, send out an APB requesting information regarding the whereabouts of Rosalind Evertsoord." He raised an index finger into the air. "And don't forget about her car," he added.

Vledder's mouth fell open.

"You're starting a case?!" he exclaimed, surprised.

The gray sleuth nodded slowly, ambled over to the coatrack, and picked up his hat from the floor.

The young inspector followed him.

"Where are you going?" he demanded.

DeKok half turned around.

"I'm going to see Dr. Aken. I want to know why a general practitioner in Purmerend refers a young woman to a neurologist in Amsterdam because of some vague complaints about being listless."

DeKok watched with admiration as the young uniformed constable guided the patrol car through the Ij
Tunnel. As he watched the traffic flowing past, sepa-
rated by what did not look like enough space, he again
congratulated himself for having had the good sense to
commandeer a patrol car, with driver. DeKok did not
like to drive. He was very aware of the simple fact that
he was probably the worst driver in the Netherlands,
maybe in all of Europe, and he avoided driving as much
as possible. But Vledder was not available, and after one
look at the old VW assigned to the team, the gray sleuth
decided that there had to be another way. The constable
had been flattered when DeKok asked him to drive to
Purmerend.

Soon they had left the city behind and were driving
alongside the North-Holland Canal, which connects the
locks of Ijmuiden, by the North Sea coast, with the inner
harbor of Amsterdam.

The constable was silent and DeKok was thoughtful.
He understood why Vledder was inclined to disbelieve
the tale told by Netherwood. On the face of it, it was
simply absurd. And the young man made a rather irreso-
lute impression. He seemed slow, almost lethargic, which
was accentuated by his gawky behavior and his loutish
clothing. It was not the sort of appearance that evoked
trust or confidence. But yet, thought DeKok, there had
been a small spark of conviction in the tale, which made
DeKok believe that there was a core of truth in the
macabre story of the sudden disappearance of Rosalind

Evertsoord. It was no more than an impression, an intuition, and he would like to have some facts to either prove or disprove his feelings.

For just a moment he had considered asking Richard Netherwood to show him his arm so he could inspect the puncture made by the needle for tapping some of his blood. It should still have been visible. But he decided that such a request was a too open sign of skepticism.

In Purmerend, the constable drove unerringly through the old center of the town, famed for its weekly cattle market, toward the new section that had been built in response to the pressures of a steadily growing Amsterdam. There they easily found Shepherds Lane, where Dr. Aken had his office.

DeKok asked the constable to turn into the first side street, where he exited the car.

"Please wait for me here," said DeKok. "I don't think I'll be long."

"Yes, sir," answered the constable. "The watch commander told me to hold myself available to you, no matter how long it took."

"Thank you," said DeKok, and turned away.

He ambled around the corner and approached number five. He pushed open the door and found a lovely nurse's assistant in the hall. She smiled and looked a question at him.

The gray sleuth lifted his hat fractionally.

"Is the doctor still here?"

"Certainly."

"Then I would like to talk to him."

"Do you have an appointment?"

DeKok shook his head.

"I'm not a patient. I'm a police inspector from Amsterdam. Perhaps the doctor can give me a few minutes?"

The assistant disappeared behind a door. After a few minutes she returned.

"Please go to the waiting room. The doctor is with a patient, but as soon as she has left, he'll be with you."

DeKok nodded and entered the waiting room. Almost immediately a young woman came out of the office. She held the door for DeKok. DeKok nodded at her and walked into the office.

Dr. Jan Aken turned out to be a tall, slender man of about forty years of age. As soon as he saw DeKok, he rose from behind his desk and extended his hand.

"What brings an Amsterdam police officer to Purmerend?" he asked jovially.

DeKok looked at him and encountered, behind thick spectacles, a friendly almost innocent look of surprise.

"Clarity," answered DeKok.

Dr. Aken laughed shyly.

"Clarity?" he repeated, puzzled.

DeKok nodded.

"You asked what an Amsterdam cop is doing in Purmerend. Well, I look for clarity in a rather strange affair, in relation to the mysterious disappearance of a young woman."

Dr. Aken offered DeKok a chair and retreated behind his desk.

"And you feel I can help you with that?" he asked, with just a hint of doubt in his voice.

The old inspector placed his hat on the floor next to his chair. Then he unbuttoned his coat. They were movements to gain time while he wondered what sort of tactic he would follow. Dr. Aken did not look like a man who would be easily impressed.

"I was hoping for your support," began DeKok carefully. "My medical knowledge is almost nonexistent. For instance, what would you do if someone came to see you with vague complaints about being listless?"

Dr. Aken moved his glasses, as if to see better.

"You have those complaints?" he asked with a smile.

DeKok gave him a searching look. Despite the obvious joviality, the look behind the glasses had changed from surprise to watchfulness and suspicion. The inspector changed direction.

"Are there any neurologists in Purmerend?"

Aken nodded with emphasis.

"We have two neurologists. They are both accredited to St. Lidwina Hospital."

"Accomplished physicians?"

"Most certainly."

DeKok grinned.

"Then why did you refer a patient residing in Purmerend to a neurologist in Amsterdam?"

The doctor frowned.

"I'm supposed to have done that?" he asked, disbelief in his voice.

DeKok leaned forward.

"You referred a patient to the neurology department of Slotervaart Hospital in Amsterdam."

"That's absurd," said the doctor, shaking his head.

DeKok looked evenly across the desk.

"Rosalind Evertsoord."

Dr. Aken frowned, as if in thought.

"Who is that?"

DeKok made an impatient gesture.

"The patient," he said, annoyed, "whom you referred two days ago to the neurology department in Amsterdam."

The face of the doctor became a frozen mask. The jovial attitude had completely disappeared. He pressed his lips together and looked hostile.

"I know no Rosalind Evertsoord," he said finally, sharply. "She is most certainly not one of my patients." He stood up from his chair. His cheeks had turned red with anger. "And I have never referred a patient to Slotervaart Hospital in Amsterdam."

Vledder had a pleased expression on his face as he looked at DeKok.

"The good doctor says he doesn't know any Rosalind Evertsoord?"

"He says she is no patient of his," confirmed DeKok.

The young inspector grinned.

"He has never referred anyone to Slotervaart Hospital in Amsterdam?"

DeKok sighed.

"When I insisted and said that he had referred Rosalind to Slotervaart, he became angry. Because I did not want to escalate the situation, I left it at that and, apparently chastised, I went away." DeKok smiled sadly. "I'd rather stay on the good side of doctors. They might just prescribe the wrong pills for you otherwise."

Vledder laughed. He moved a chair closer to DeKok's desk and seated himself backward, his arms leaning on the back of the chair.

"Didn't I say so right away? Didn't I say I wouldn't give a wooden nickel for that story of Richard Netherwood?"

DeKok pursed his lips.

"I found his description of the happenings in Slotervaart Hospital quite convincing, realistic, and very detailed."

Vledder grinned broadly.

"But pure invention from beginning to end."

DeKok looked surprised.

"Why do you say that?"

Vledder looked serious.

"Richard Netherwood suffers from hallucinations and paranoia."

"What?"

"He suffers from a personality disorder that results in hallucinations and a feeling of persecution. As a rule, people with this condition can function in society, but their behavior is sometimes rather, eh, confusing."

DeKok leaned his head to one side.

"And where did you gain all that wisdom?"

"From Dr. Bemmel."

DeKok narrowed his eyes.

"Who is Dr. Bemmel?"

"The big boss. The chief surgeon and director of Slotervaart Hospital."

"And he knows Richard Netherwood?"

"Not really."

"So how can he say what he said?"

Vledder sighed.

"As you instructed me, this morning I called Sloter-vaart Hospital and asked to be connected to the chief administrator. I was connected to Dr. Bemmel. I asked for an interview and he asked, with some justification, I might add, in what context I wanted an interview." Vledder grimaced. "Well, then I told him about Richard Netherwood and the fact that his girlfriend had been lost in the hospital last Wednesday."

"How did he react?"

"Dr. Bemmel laughed and said that he would check with the morgue to see if a corpse had been misplaced."

DeKok shook his head.

"A macabre joke," he said disapprovingly, "not worthy of a chief surgeon." He looked at Vledder. "If I understand you correctly, Dr. Bemmel did not take your story seriously?"

"On the contrary. He said his schedule was rather full and that he had no time in the immediate future for an interview with us, but that he would give instruction that the personnel of the hospital should fully cooperate with us. He also promised to send us a duty roster so we could see who was on duty that morning."

"Very good."

Vledder nodded agreement.

"I thought so. But Dr. Bemmel advised us not to pay too much attention to the story of the young man. He warned us specifically that paranoid people often have the gift of being able to present their hallucinations in a very convincing manner."

DeKok rubbed the back of his neck.

"But is Richard a paranoid personality?"

Vledder spread both arms.

"It is possible," he said. "It offers a reasonable explanation for the strange tale he told us."

DeKok looked up.

"And he told the same story at Slotermeer Station?"

Vledder nodded.

"Almost verbatim."

"And?"

The young inspector shrugged his shoulders.

"Our colleagues at Slotermeer reacted as I did."

"They didn't take it seriously?"

Vledder shook his head slowly.

"They did nothing in response to his story and called you crazy for going to Purmerend to talk to that Dr. Aken."

DeKok grinned.

"It isn't the first time," he said resignedly.

"What?"

"That I have been called crazy."

The telephone on DeKok's desk rang. Vledder reached over and answered it. The message was not long. After about a minute he replaced the receiver. His face was pale.

"They found her car."

"Who? Where?"

"Divers. In the North-Holland Canal."

"And what about Rosie?"

"Her body has not yet been found."

3

"Do you have all the details?"

Vledder pushed his notes together in a pile and logged on to his computer.

"Captain Jelle Jaarsma," he read from the screen, "skipper of the motorized barge *Three Brothers*, felt a bump when sailing along the North-Holland Canal. He knew he could not have touched bottom, so suspected an underwater obstacle of some kind. He was, at that time, in the shallow channel of the canal." He looked up and added, "There are three channels in the canal. The center channel is for oceangoing vessels and the two shallow channels are for barge traffic going east and west, outside the buoyed path of the larger ships."

DeKok nodded with some impatience and motioned for him to continue.

"The skipper alerted the lockkeeper, who informed the police. Two divers from the Ijmuiden police went into the water at the indicated place and found a car. A crane, supplied by the local fire station, raised the vehicle and upon investigation found the car to have been registered in the name of Rosalind Evertsoord."

"There was no body in the car?"

Vledder shook his head.

"No sign of a driver or a passenger," he confirmed. "Both doors were open. According to the divers, it is possible that the body—or bodies—may have been sucked out of the car because of the current created by passing ships. The body may be anywhere on the bottom of the canal."

DeKok scratched the back of his neck.

"Was the car damaged?"

"You mean, did it wind up in the canal because of a collision?"

"Exactly."

Vledder shook his head.

"There was some damage, but according to the Ijmuiden police that was caused by the *Three Brothers* as she scraped the vehicle."

"Not a clue about a cause?"

"Not a one. No skid marks…nothing. The place where the car was found is near a quay that's used for loading and unloading, but mainly for barges to tie up temporarily. There is no railing there."

"Witnesses?"

Vledder shook his head again.

"No witnesses, no reports from passing motorists about something suspicious."

"A strange case."

Vledder shrugged his shoulders.

"I don't think it's all that strange. Almost daily people wind up in a canal and drown. In Amsterdam alone they recover at least one car a day from the water. There is a lot of water in the Netherlands." He paused. "When her body surfaces, in a day or so, we can cancel the APB."

DeKok shook his head in disapproval.

"And close the file on Rosalind Evertsoord?"

Vledder nodded.

"There's nothing left to investigate. She drove back to her flat in Purmerend and wound up in the North-Holland Canal somehow."

"In broad daylight?"

Vledder reacted with some irritation.

"In the evening, who knows? In any case, it seems clear to me that there is no question of a disappearance as Richard Netherwood wants us to believe. And it has nothing to do with Slotervaart Hospital."

DeKok pushed out his lower lip and let it plop back. It was one of his more unpleasant habits.

"A premature conclusion."

Vledder looked surprised.

"Why premature?"

The gray sleuth closed his eyes for a second.

"You see," he said thoughtfully, "the body of that young woman has not yet surfaced."

From Warmoes Street the two inspectors ambled through the quarter toward Front Fort Canal. As usual, it was bustling in the Red Light District. Men waited in queues in front of the numerous porno theaters and sex shops. Tourists giggled and ogled the women in the windows.

"Have you informed Richard Netherwood that we found Rosie's car?" DeKok asked, indifferent to his immodest surroundings.

The young inspector shook his head.

"I haven't," he said mulishly.

"Why not?"

Vledder glanced aside. There was an angry blush on his cheeks.

"It may very well be that you have a limitless trust in that young man, but I don't. We need to keep in mind that he may have had something to do with the sinking of her car."

DeKok looked surprised.

"Sinking?" he asked. "And I thought you wanted to drop the entire case?"

Vledder sighed deeply.

"I've been thinking. You're right, it's strange. Rosalind Evertsoord has been living in Purmerend for several years. It is to be expected that she's very much aware of the traffic situation around that town." The young inspector stood suddenly still. "Just think, why would Richard Netherwood approach us with that strange tale about his Rosie? Why would he draw our attention particularly to Slotervaart Hospital?"

"Because that is where he lost her."

Vledder shook his head and walked away.

"Nonsense. It's a diversion."

"For what?"

"For his own behavior."

DeKok pushed back his hat.

"I don't follow."

Vledder raised a forefinger and used it to tap the side of his nose. He resumed his slow pace.

"Presume," he said didactically, "that Richard knew that Rosie wanted to break off the relationship, that she had found someone else." He grinned widely. "For a less-than-attractive man such as Richard, that may be tragic."

"And?"

Vledder stopped again.

"Let's assume that Richard simply could not stand the thought that he would have to relinquish Rosie to another."

DeKok looked at his young partner with surprise.

"Are you saying that Rosie's car did not end up in the canal as the result of an accident?"

Vledder nodded.

"It was murder."

"Ingenious, but I would not be too hasty to assume murder, my friend."

"You have your opinions, I have mine," Vledder remarked over his shoulder.

Just past Old Church Square at the corner of St. Anne Alley, DeKok and Vledder came across a group of curious onlookers watching a drunk repeatedly trying to embrace a young prostitute. Although the young woman tried to fight him off, the man stubbornly continued his attempts. Only after she received assistance from a few of her sisters in the business did the man stagger away, cursing.

After making sure the woman was unharmed and safe, the inspectors continued on, crossing the bridge near Steam Alley and arriving at Little Lowee's establishment.

"Shouldn't we have stepped in?" asked Vledder as they pushed aside the heavy curtain inside the door.

"No," answered DeKok dispassionately. "The quarter corrects those situations by itself. You may have noticed nobody was calling for the police."

Lowee, regularly referred to as Little Lowee, heard the end of DeKok's sentence.

"Whafor shoulda call da cops?" he wanted to know.

"Nothing, Lowee," said DeKok as he hoisted himself onto his favorite bar stool at the end of the bar, his back to the wall.

"Allrights, but welcome anyways," said Lowee.

DeKok grinned.

"Thanks," he said. "We're in need of a soothing drink."

Vledder sat down on the stool next to DeKok. Lowee ignored him and addressed the old inspector.

"Same recipe?" he asked.

"If you please," answered DeKok.

He looked around. It was rather quiet in the intimate bar. Most of the tables were empty. In the back a woman sat close to a heavyset businessman. It would not be long before they would retreat to her room.

Lowee produced a bottle and three snifters. With a practiced movement he removed the cork and poured a little in one of the glasses. Then he filled the other two glasses and slid them in front of Vledder and DeKok. He finished filling the first glass and put the bottle aside. Lifting his glass, he looked at DeKok with a happy smile on his face.

"*Proost*," he said.

Vledder and DeKok lifted their glasses and returned the sentiment. DeKok took a careful sip, savoring the taste of the cognac as it rolled around in his mouth. Slowly he swallowed, enjoying every second.

"Busy?" asked Lowee.

DeKok took another, bigger sip before answering.

"As usual," he said finally. "There's never a recession in crime. In the old days people used to steal because they were poor. Now they steal because they want more. That's the only difference."

Lowee gave him a searching look.

"A bit somber, ain't ya?"

DeKok smiled.

"No, I'm not somber, Lowee. When I was young, my mother had to refuse me a slice of bread from time to time. I'm sure it hurt her, but she simply did not have it." He fell silent and stared into the distance. "But who can possibly have a reason nowadays to steal bread?"

Lowee cocked his head.

"But you're kinda sad anyway, ain't ye?"

The gray sleuth waved it away.

"Why don't you pour one more time," he said, evading the question.

Lowee drained his own glass and hastened to comply with the request.

DeKok picked up his refilled glass and cradled it in his hand as he inhaled the heady perfume of the golden liquid. He took another careful sip, fully appreciating the bouquet of the fine cognac.

"Somethin' special cookin'?" asked Lowee.

DeKok stared into his glass.

"Why do you think that?"

Little Lowee made a vague gesture.

"I can smell it," he said emphatically. "Iffen youse gotta distant look inna yer glimmers, there is something' special goin'. Ain't I right?"

DeKok smiled. He felt in an inside pocket and produced the photograph of Rosalind Evertsoord and placed it in front of the barkeeper.

"You know her?"

Lowee leaned forward.

"I gotta know 'er?" he asked.

DeKok grinned at the reaction.

"It's not necessary," he answered, shaking his head. "And to tell you the truth, Lowee, I don't expect you to know her. I don't think she's the kind of woman that you'll see in this neighborhood."

The small man studied the photo with renewed interest.

"Are ye lookin' for 'er?"

"Yes."

"What for?"

"She's gone...disappeared. It's possible that she is at the bottom of the North-Holland Canal. But her friend tells me he lost her in Slotervaart Hospital."

A pained look showed on Lowee's friendly, mousy face.

"Slotervaart Hospital, you say?" He sounded amazed.

DeKok nodded.

"That's what her friend told me."

"Him, too," said Lowee.

DeKok looked puzzled.

"What do you mean?"

Little Lowee spread wide his short arms.

"Bad Bertus."

"What's the matter with him?"

"He also done 'lost' a Sheila inna da same hospital."

After they left Lowee's, they walked back via Rear Fort Canal. The district was a lot busier now. The sex business was in full swing.

Vledder looked a bit depressed. There was a worried look on his young face. He glanced aside at DeKok, who, with his decrepit hat pushed far back on his head, looked like he had not a care in the world.

"It can't be true," said Vledder.

"What?"

"About that girl of Bad Bertus."

"You mean that she, too, disappeared from Slotervaart Hospital?"

"It's just too crazy," Vledder said excitedly. "And I refuse to believe it. The hospitals in our country have a good reputation."

DeKok shrugged his shoulders.

"*Credo quia absurdum est*...I believe it because it is absurd."

"What do you mean by that?"

"A policeman should be open to all possibilities."

Vledder was not convinced.

"Do you know Bad Bertus?"

DeKok gave him a mischievous look.

"You want to know if he suffers from hallucinations?"

Vledder nodded emphatically.

"Surely that is one of the possibilities a policeman should be open to."

"Touché," said DeKok. "But to answer your question: Bertus is an aging procurer. He got his nickname in his younger days. Now he could be described as a fatherly pimp."

"Do they exist?"

"Certainly."

"And he has all his marbles?"

DeKok laughed.

"The times our paths have crossed, he has always been a little bit smarter than I."

"Of what was he suspected?"

"Black market stuff, dealing in just about anything that was profitable, regardless of the legality—antiques, art, you name it. And of course, he lived off prostitution. But as far as I know, no woman has ever filed a complaint against him."

"Because of fear?"

DeKok shook his head.

"Because the women had no reason to complain about him. He treated them right...friendly, protective, as I said, fatherly."

They walked on for a while in silence, across the bridge near Old Acquaintance Alley toward Front Fort Canal. DeKok stopped in front of green lacquered door.

Vledder looked surprised.

"What are we doing here?"

DeKok thumbed at the door.

"The residence of Bad Bertus."

The gray sleuth was amused as he looked at the man before
him. Bad Bertus wore a red velvet smoking jacket richly
decorated with gold brocade. His hairy chest was adorned
with a heavy gold chain from which a gold medallion
was suspended. The man slowly sank back down into his
recliner and looked up.

"Have you come to arrest me?"

DeKok shook his head. He pulled up a leather hassock
and sat down across from the pimp.

"No," he said in a friendly tone of voice. "I'm with
homicide now and you've never had anything to do
with that." He paused and studied the effect of his words.
"This," he continued, "is just a friendly visit."

Bad Bertus grinned.

"I can't say that I'm used to that from a cop," he
growled.

DeKok did not react. He continued to study the face of
the man. Bad Bertus, he decided, looked good. A slightly
round face, wavy gray hair, an alert look in his clear blue
eyes. The inspector waved in the direction of Vledder.

"My colleague and I are investigating the sudden disappearance of a young woman."

"And what does that have to do with me?"

DeKok smiled.

"Nothing—that is, as far as we know. The young woman
disappeared a few days ago in Slotervaart Hospital and we
found her car in the North-Holland Canal." He paused,
pulled out his lower lip, and let it plop back. "According to
our information," he continued after a while, "you had a

similar experience. It is being said that, eh, a...one of your acquaintances disappeared in Slotervaart Hospital."

Bertus nodded.

"Annie, Annie Scheepstra." He leaned farther back in his chair, thereby showing a lot more of his hairy chest. "But you have to understand, I don't really know if she disappeared in that hospital. I just never seen her again."

DeKok stretched out a finger toward the man.

"Were you with her?"

"What do you mean?"

"Were you with her in the hospital when she disappeared?"

Bad Bertus raised his hands in a defensive gesture.

"Take it easy, will you? You have to give me time to explain." He moved in his chair and adjusted his jacket. "Annie Scheepstra has been with me for a while," he started. "I got her a room just around the corner. She did very well. She was attractive and friendly. But she was a hummingbird, you know, restless. You could never depend on her. Sometimes she disappeared for a few days at a time and then she would return. The last time she came back, she had a boy with her...an athlete, you know, some self-absorbed bodybuilder, or an amateur boxer, who knows...someone who only thought of himself."

"I know the type," said DeKok. "Go on."

"Well, she went to live with him in an apartment in Purmerend. It didn't bother me, to tell you the truth, it was just one of those things. You know yourself how these girls are, and I have never believed in force. Sooner or later they come back. They just can't get used to a normal life."

DeKok nodded his understanding.

"You kept in contact with her?"

Bertus shook his head.

"Not really. You can't chase these broads all the time. But a few days ago, Annie called me early in the morning and she said, 'Bep,' they call me Bep, you see. Anyway, she said, 'Bep, I have to go to the hospital in Amsterdam. Will you come with me?'"

"And?"

Bad Bertus spread his arms.

"I was a bit shocked, as you can understand. I asked her what was the matter, was she sick? Did she need an operation? But she told me there was actually not much the matter with her, but she was listless and tired. That's why she went to the doctor, who gave her a referral to Slotervaart Hospital."

DeKok gestured impatiently.

"Did you go with her?"

Bertus nodded.

"Of course I went with her. You don't abandon a child like that, now do you? I picked her up at Central Station and from there we took a taxi to the hospital. While I took care of the cabdriver, Annie gave her referral to somebody at the counter. Within a few minutes a nurse came to get her."

DeKok gave him a searching look.

"Did you notice the nurse?"

Bertus grinned.

"You think I was looking for new talent for one of my rooms?"

DeKok shook his head.

"Never mind that. What did she look like?"

Bertus gestured nonchalantly.

"I don't know. In those hospitals they all look alike, and this one did not look any different."

DeKok looked disappointed.

"What else?"

Bertus suddenly looked a bit helpless.

"Nothing else. I sat there for about an hour and a half in the waiting area. Then I had enough. I left. There's a bus stop in front. I took the bus to Damrak and then walked home."

"And what about Annie?"

Bertus shrugged.

"I have not seen her again."

DeKok looked puzzled.

"You didn't ask around in the hospital trying to find out what had happened to her?"

Bad Bertus shook his head.

"I'm not that crazy about hospitals. I've never been a patient in one and I hope I never will be. The smell is enough to make you sick and I don't trust those guys in their white coats."

DeKok grinned disbelievingly.

"Have you notified the police of her, eh, of her disappearance?"

Bertus reacted peevishly.

"Ach, that broad will turn up one of these days. Before you know it, she'll be at my door asking to come back."

DeKok looked at him sharply.

"Did Annie show you the referral to the hospital?"

Bertus nodded.

"I seen it."

DeKok tensed inside, but outwardly he remained calm.

"Do you happen to remember which doctor signed the referral?"

"Yeah, Annie was completely besotted with him. She found him to be a fine, understanding man."

"Who?"

"That Dr. Aken."

4

_____

Slowly rocking on the balls of his feet, DeKok stood in front of the window and looked out over the rooftops of the Red Light District. He was deep in thought. Down in the street a drunk sang a sad song of lost love. A uniformed constable led him to the sidewalk, but took no further action. DeKok silently approved of the restraint shown by the young police officer. There were more important things to be worried about.

Many times he had stood like this in front of the window, pondering a case while observing the quarter. It helped him think.

Suddenly he realized that it was just three days to the start of Sail Amsterdam. Just three days until the tall ships entered the harbor. Just three days to solve the mystery of the disappearing women. He wondered if it was enough time. Vledder broke in on his musings.

"Didn't you go and see Aken in Purmerend?"

"Yes, I went to his office."

"What sort of man is he?"

DeKok shrugged.

"Just a man in a white coat, the ubiquitous stethoscope around his neck. I could detect nothing suspicious about him." He frowned. Vledder watched the ripple of

DeKok's eyebrows with fascination. They took on a life of their own and seemed to actually dance on his forehead. As soon as the phenomenon had started it was over, and Vledder wondered, not for the first time, if he really could have seen what he thought he saw.

"But doctors and crime," continued DeKok thoughtfully. "Just read any good piece of fiction. They are a common combination, and we have had a few encounters with that duo ourselves."

Vledder nodded.

DeKok gave his young partner a sharp look.

"But I thought you weren't interested in this case?"

Vledder came from behind his desk and stood next to his mentor.

"Of course I'm interested. After we found Rosalind's car in the canal, I became convinced that something happened to her. And I think that Annie Scheepstra is in danger as well. If she had not arrived in Amsterdam by train, we would probably have found her car in the canal, too." The young inspector gestured agitatedly. "I just don't believe those absurd stories...neither Richard Netherwood's, nor that one from Bad Bertus."

"Why not?"

Vledder shook his head.

"This is Holland. People don't disappear in hospitals." He grinned wryly. "Not even in psychiatric hospitals."

DeKok glanced aside.

"And you don't think Dr. Aken is involved?"

Vledder grimaced.

"Both women lived in Purmerend and had the same doctor. What's so unusual about that?"

DeKok sighed deeply.

"The unusual thing," said DeKok, "is the fact that Dr. Aken positively denies that he referred Rosalind Evertsoord to Slotervaart Hospital. That bothers me. If he did not do that, then—"

Vledder interrupted.

"Then that leaves just one option."

"And what is that?"

Vledder gesticulated wildly.

"We ask Dr. Aken if he knows Annie Scheepstra...if he referred her to Slotervaart Hospital. The man must be a real unscrupulous liar if he denies that as well."

"But they exist."

"What?"

"Unscrupulous liars."

Vledder bit his lip.

"But this time we have a witness, a witness who saw the referral."

"Bad Bertus."

"Exactly."

DeKok glanced at the large clock on the wall. It was almost eleven o'clock.

"You want to go to Purmerend now?" he asked.

Vledder nodded with emphasis.

"We don't have a lot of time." He pointed at the window. "You want to go to Sail Amsterdam, don't you?"

DeKok smiled.

"Yes, I do. And I thank you for keeping that in mind."

Vledder drove the old police VW a bit too fast along the road that had once been a tow path for horses pulling barges. The abused engine groaned and the almost non-existent suspension made sure the passengers felt every bump in the road. DeKok endured it stoically for a while. Then he sank down in the seat and made himself as comfortable as possible.

"Twice a day to Purmerend is a bit much, I think," he grunted.

Vledder laughed.

"If you had been a bit more forceful with Dr. Aken this morning, this trip would not be necessary."

DeKok snorted.

"What would you have me do? Use thumbscrews? Roast him over an open fire?" His voice vibrated with sarcasm. "He told me that Rosalind Evertsoord was no patient of his and that he did not refer her to Slotervaart Hospital. That was the end of his story."

"And you believed him?"

A pained expression fled across DeKok's face.

"If we assume that Dr. Aken was lying, that he had referred Rosalind to an Amsterdam hospital, then we have to ask ourselves, Why did he lie? I have to confess that I have no answer to that question. I can't imagine what he hoped to gain by that."

"But this time we can confront him with Bad Bertus's story."

DeKok sighed and shook his head.

"I'm afraid it won't help much."

Vledder looked surprised.

"Surely you don't think that he'll say that Annie

Scheepstra is no patient of his and that he never referred her to Slotervaart Hospital?"

"That's what I think, yes."

Vledder took one hand from the steering wheel and slapped the dashboard.

"But that's impossible. It's just too crazy!"

DeKok nodded slowly to himself.

"You're right, that's what it is. The whole case is just too crazy." He scratched the back of his neck. "If the director of the hospital provides us with the duty roster, then we'll have to stage a reenactment."

Vledder frowned.

"What sort of reenactment?"

DeKok sighed.

"A lineup. We take Richard Netherwood to the hospital and summon the personnel who were on duty at the time of Rosalind's disappearance."

"Then what?"

"Then that young man can point out the nurse who took Rosalind away and did not bring her back."

Vledder grimaced.

"So you're determined to investigate the hospital?"

DeKok nodded.

"If you're right," he said calmly, "if the hospital has nothing to do with the disappearance of those two women, the investigation will make that clear."

Vledder shook his head.

"You don't need an investigation for that," he growled. "Silly and superfluous. The very thought is silly." He paused and stared at the road with an angry look on his face. "And what about Bad Bertus?"

DeKok smiled.

"I don't think we can count on his cooperation," he said with a sigh. "Annie's disappearance hardly touches him. There are plenty of women available for his sex business. Besides, Bertus doesn't like hospitals. A few years back some competing pimps beat him up rather severely, but Bertus refused to be taken to a hospital. I was there when they found him in an alley. I remember he said, 'I'd rather die than go to a hospital.' So we took him home and he fixed himself up somehow."

Vledder slowed down as they entered Purmerend. He glanced aside.

"Where do you want to go?"

DeKok straightened up and took a piece of paper from his chest pocket. He smoothed it out and studied it.

"According to my information, Dr. Aken lives on Captains Way, but I think we better go to his office first."

"On Shepherds Lane?"

"Yes."

"You think he'll still be there, at this hour?"

DeKok shook his head.

"I don't think so. But I think his charming assistant lives on the ground floor, next to the office. We can ask her how to reach the good doctor."

They drove slowly on through the neighborhood and parked the VW in front of a large apartment building. From there they walked to Shepherds Lane. They stopped in front of a door. Next to it, a sign announced office hours. DeKok rang the doorbell. A few minutes later the door opened and they were confronted by an attractive young woman dressed in a white blouse with wide sleeves and a pair of Levis. She looked at her visitors with a questioning look on her face.

DeKok politely lifted his hat.

"Do you remember me? I was here this morning."

She cocked her head.

"You're with the police...from Amsterdam."

DeKok smiled.

"Very good," he said with a hint of admiration in his voice. "There have been a few new developments in our investigation. Therefore we wanted to consult with Dr. Aken again."

The young woman shook her head.

"That's impossible."

"Why?"

"The doctor is away."

DeKok was taken aback.

"Away, you say?"

The young woman nodded.

"This afternoon, by plane."

"Where to?"

"Sri Lanka, for three weeks."

In silence and with somber faces, the two inspectors drove back to Amsterdam. The sudden departure of Dr. Aken for faraway Sri Lanka had dumfounded them. Just to be sure, they had stopped by Captains Way. When they rang the doorbell, there was no answer. The villa seemed deserted.

There was relatively little traffic on the way back. An occasional bus passed them in the HOV lane. Close to the city, it started to rain. Streams of water skidded across the windshield. Vledder turned on the wipers. DeKok stared out of the window, fighting the urge to move his head along with the compelling rhythm of the wipers. After a while he covered his eyes by pushing his hat forward.

"Three weeks," he growled. "I can't keep the case open for that long." A grin played around his mouth. "I'm afraid the commissaris will not give us permission to travel to Sri Lanka."

Vledder gripped the steering wheel with renewed force.

"Did you believe that assistant?"

"That Dr. Aken was depressed by his busy practice? That he was on the verge of a nervous breakdown?"

Vledder grinned wryly.

"Yes, and therefore he packed his bags and took off for a three-week vacation in Sri Lanka." He shook his head. "I just don't believe it. A departure like that takes some preparation. One doesn't do that from one moment to the next. I think that Dr. Aken has fled the country."

DeKok shrugged.

"Flee? Why?"

Vledder slapped the steering wheel with a flat hand.

"Fleeing from us! A fugitive from justice...to avoid a possible arrest." He reacted venomously. "Your visit this morning must have made him realize that the case was developing."

The gray sleuth pushed back his little hat and glanced at his partner.

"What case?" he asked innocently.

Vledder swallowed.

"The case of the disappearing women."

For a while DeKok made no comment.

"How," he asked finally, slowly, "would you describe his complicity in this crime?"

Vledder paused in turn. His face became pensive.

"That I don't know," he confessed after a while. "Not yet. I don't know enough. I don't know where he fits in."

DeKok grinned broadly.

"And you talk of a fugitive from justice to avoid a possible arrest? For just a moment I believed that you had discovered an illegal action." The old man's tone was cynical.

Vledder reacted curtly.

"I was looking for a motive for his flight," he defended himself. "That's all. I admit that we have no idea how closely the doctor is involved. But in view of his hasty departure, I think that his involvement is possibly greater than we at first suspected."

DeKok sighed.

"That's wishful thinking."

"Why do you say that?"

"Let me try to explain," said DeKok patiently. "Because there are few leads, you wish the involvement of Dr. Aken. You wish that he had something to do with the disappearance of the young women. And because you wish that, you explain his vacation in Sri Lanka as a flight from justice, and as a consequence you're looking for motives for that flight that fit your theory, your wishes. That's wishful thinking, and a bad habit to get into for a police officer."

There was a stubborn look on Vledder's face. DeKok studied it and sighed.

"Look, Dick," he said, "everybody has days when they wish they could escape from work or personal life. And

why should Dr. Aken not be close to a nervous breakdown? I think he has indeed a busy practice."

Vledder pressed his lips together. His face was expressionless and red spots appeared on his cheeks.

"It was a flight."

It sounded uncompromising.

DeKok slid back down in the seat and remained silent.

Vledder parked the VW behind the station. Down Old
Bridge Alley they walked back to Warmoes Street. It was
late afternoon and the crowds had thinned out a bit. The
quarter was gathering its strength for the onslaught to come
later in the evening. They entered the station house.

Jan Kusters, the watch commander, called out that
somebody was waiting for them upstairs.

DeKok glanced at the clock.

"A bit late, isn't it?"

The watch commander nodded.

"He came in about an hour ago and asked for you."

"Who?"

Kusters consulted his logbook.

"Paul Voldrop."

"Means nothing to me."

"Well, he asked for you. He says that a prostitute has
been murdered…a certain Annie Scheepstra."

"What?"

Kusters nodded.

"He claims to know why."

5

As Vledder and DeKok reached the top of the stairs, a young man hastily got up from the bench in the corridor. The old inspector studied him carefully. He guessed him to be in his mid-twenties. Well built, with a short neck, wide shoulders, and narrow hips. The body of a boxer. The results of years of bodybuilding were evident.

His clothes were garish, almost laughable. Especially his wide jacket of rough tweed decorated with huge yellow squares that reminded one of a clown's costume.

The young man approached the inspectors, nervously running his fingers inside the neck of his shirt.

"Are you Inspector DeKok?"

The gray sleuth nodded.

"With, eh, a kay-oh-kay," he said automatically.

The man bit his lower lip.

"I've been waiting at least an hour."

DeKok smiled.

"I admire your tenacity," he said. "And your patience. I presume, therefore, that you have an important message."

"Yes, I have," nodded the young man.

DeKok passed him and entered the detective room. Voldrop and Vledder followed. With old-fashioned courtesy,

DeKok bowed in the direction of the chair next to his desk.

"Please, have a seat," DeKok said while he divested himself of his dilapidated little hat and wrinkled raincoat. Then he sat down behind his desk, an expression of good-will on his face.

"Who are you?" he asked in a friendly tone of voice.

The young man undid the buttons of his jacket.

"Paul, Paul Voldrop."

"Have you ever been in contact with the police?"

He shook his head.

"So far, I've managed to stay out of the greedy clutches of the judiciary."

DeKok grinned.

"Who told you about me?"

Voldrop nodded in the direction of the window.

"Blond Mina."

"And who is Blond Mina?"

"A working girl in the neighborhood."

"And you have a relationship with her?"

Paul Voldrop shook his head.

"Not me. Not really, I mean. Blond Mina is an acquaintance of my girlfriend, Annie Scheepstra. They did work together, in the past…and made a lot of money," he added sheepishly.

"And Blond Mina mentioned my name?"

The young man nodded.

"She told me to come here and ask for Inspector DeKok. She thought that was better."

DeKok looked a question.

"Better than what?"

"Than to mess with it myself."

DeKok gave him a sharp look.

"You're speaking in riddles. Mess with what?"

"The disappearance of Annie. I wanted to investigate that. But Blond Mina told me that it was dangerous to try that on my own." He suddenly looked at DeKok. "You... eh, you do know that Annie has suddenly disappeared?"

The gray sleuth nodded slowly.

"I've known for several hours."

"Who told you?"

DeKok rubbed his nose with a little finger.

"Somebody of no consequence," he evaded.

Paul Voldrop licked dry lips.

"Annie and I have been living together for some time, at least two months. I met her at a party for our club." He patted his wide chest with the tips of his fingers. "I box. A few years ago I almost made Champion of North-Holland. Welterweight. Annie is fascinated with boxing. Her father used to box. That's why she was invited to the party. I liked her immediately. I had somebody introduce me and asked her out." He grinned boyishly. "She agreed. The very next day we met in Amsterdam. After going out to a club and dinner, she told me she had had a bad upbringing and was involved with prostitution."

DeKok gave him another sharp look.

"How did you react?"

Paul moved uncertainly in his chair.

"I, eh, I was a bit upset. I didn't know what to say. She didn't look like a whore, not at all. After I got over the shock, I asked what she wanted to do...if she wanted to continue as a prostitute. She looked at me and laughed. She said that she would give it up if she found a suitable guy."

"And you're a suitable guy?"

"So she said."

"Then what?"

"She moved in with me. I have a two-bedroom apartment in Purmerend, very nice, in a large apartment building. Cozy and plenty of room. Annie was quite happy there."

DeKok nodded.

"And then she said she felt a bit depressed and listless and went to see Dr. Aken."

Paul Voldrop looked surprised.

"How do you know that?" he asked.

DeKok did not answer the question.

"Was she listless?"

The young man shrugged his broad shoulders.

"I didn't notice anything." He smiled and continued. "Annie...I sometimes had trouble following her tempo. She was a real live wire."

"But she went to see Dr. Aken?"

"Yeah."

"Why?"

Voldrop spread his arms in a gesture of surrender.

"I don't know," he exclaimed, desperation in his voice. "She said she felt down, real tired. How can I judge that? It's her body, not mine."

DeKok ignored the remark.

"What did Dr. Aken say?"

"He examined her and told her to go to Slotervaart Hospital."

"Did you see the referral?"

The young man nodded.

"Neurology department, it said on the envelope, to the attention of Dr. Lesterhuis."

DeKok narrowed his eyes.

"Dr. Lesterhuis?"

Paul Voldrop nodded again.

"That's what the scribbles from Dr. Aken seemed to say. Maybe it was Nesterhuis, or Lesterheem. It was hard to make out, doctor's handwriting and all."

"Was there anything in the referral about the kind of illness or disease for which Dr. Aken referred her?"

"I didn't open the envelope."

DeKok used the little finger of his other hand to rub his nose.

"Why didn't you go to the hospital with her?"

"She preferred Bad Bertus," Voldrop said bitterly. "She clearly trusted that dirty pimp more than she did me."

"And you never saw her again?"

"No."

"Any idea where she might be?"

Voldrop shrugged his shoulders.

"In heaven, or in hell."

"What do you mean?"

"I mean she's dead."

DeKok suddenly stood up, ignoring the young man, and started to pace up and down the detective room. Vledder was familiar with the habit, but still was fascinated by the way DeKok navigated the busy room, his brain churning at full speed. Vledder wondered what his old partner had heard or deduced. He shrugged. He would find out soon enough.

DeKok's thoughts went over the facts he had so far. Paul Voldrop, he mused, could be of prime importance to the investigation, a vital link in the chain of events. It was senseless to overwhelm him with questions, which is why he had interrupted the interrogation. He wanted the young man to calm down and reflect...reflect on the accusations that DeKok felt intuitively were bound to follow. DeKok was not in need of wild accusations. Proof, incontrovertible proof, that is what a Dutch judge demanded. And it was his task, as a police officer, to supply that proof. It had been his task for a long time.

He glanced at the clock. It was well past midnight. Suddenly he felt his age and wished he hadn't ignored that inner voice this morning tempting him away from his duty. With a sad smile on his face, he walked back to his desk and sat down.

"Dead, you say?"

Voldrop nodded.

"That's what I said."

DeKok leaned his head to one side.

"Is there a reason for this assumption?"

The young man nodded emphatically.

"She has been murdered."

DeKok's expression did not change.

"Who did it?"

Paul sat up straight in his chair and stuck out his chin.

"Bad Bertus."

DeKok did not react. He searched his own feelings and found that the accusation did not shock him. He had expected that answer, more or less. He rubbed his face with a flat hand and looked at the man.

"My colleague Vledder and I," he said pensively, "talked with Bad Bertus for some time earlier today."

"About Annie?"

"Yes."

Voldrop gave him an intense look.

"What did he say?"

DeKok made a nonchalant gesture.

"He picked up Annie, at her request, at Central Station and then took her in a cab to the hospital. At the hospital, Annie gave Dr. Aken's referral to someone at the desk and a nurse came to get her."

"And?"

"And?" DeKok copied.

Voldrop looked impatient.

"What happened next?"

DeKok sighed deeply.

"She did not return," he answered. "Bertus waited for about an hour and a half and then went home on a bus."

"Without Annie?"

"Yes."

Voldrop grinned.

"And you believe that?" he asked sarcastically.

DeKok shrugged.

"That was his story."

The young man leaned forward.

"Well, let me tell you something," he lectured. "Annie was never in the hospital...she never made it there."

DeKok frowned. For a moment Paul Voldrop was taken aback. Then he shook his head, as if to clear his vision. DeKok's eyebrows had made their usual dance. DeKok acted as if nothing had happened.

"How did you come to that conclusion?" he asked.

Paul Voldrop thumbed over his shoulder.

"I've been to that hospital. I inquired. They checked the entire administration for me. Nobody had heard anything about a Miss Scheepstra. Her name did not appear in any register. So you see, Annie never went to the hospital." He paused, took a deep breath. "If I were you," he continued with conviction, "I'd go back to Bad Bertus and ask him what happened to Annie."

DeKok looked at the man before him. The ugly yellow color of the jacket hurt his eyes. His mood became hostile. He did not like to be lectured.

"You do not decide what I have to do," he said icily.

The young man grinned.

"And yet it seems to me a good idea to ask Bertus some hard questions. For instance, what happened to the little book?"

"What little book?"

Voldrop looked at him evenly.

"About the miracle."

6

Paul Voldrop stomped out of the room after reluctantly telling the story of the book. With the exit of the hideously bright jacket, it suddenly seemed as if all color had left the detective room. While the echo of his heavy tread still filled the air, the two inspectors looked at each other. Both pale, sleep-deprived faces showed an expression of surprise and bewilderment.

Vledder looked quizzically at his old partner.

"Is Bad Bertus a murderer?"

DeKok sank back in his chair.

"I don't think so," he sighed. "I've never even heard a rumor to that effect. You've met him yourself...he comes across as a pleasant, mild-mannered man." He shrugged his shoulders. "But money, money is an instrument of the devil."

Vledder narrowed his eyes.

"A murder for hire?"

"Exactly."

The young inspector pressed his lips together, disapproval on his face.

"You think that a book about a miracle is really worth that much?" he asked, wondering. "I mean, enough so that Bertus can afford to hire a killer?"

"And have something left?"

"Indeed."

DeKok made a helpless gesture.

"What do I know about antiques?" he exclaimed, exasperated. "I know that some paintings can bring fabulous prices, but a book about miracles…"

He did not finish the sentence, but looked at Vledder.

"Did you take notes?"

"Of course," he said as he patted his computer screen affectionately.

"Give me a synopsis."

Vledder touched some keys and then began to read from his screen.

"Annie Scheepstra," he began, "has, or rather had, an uncle by the name of Arnold Vreeden. The oldest brother of her deceased mother. Mr. Vreeden was director of a Christian school community in Amsterdam. At age sixty he was thanked for his services and started drawing a pension. A few years ago, shortly after the death of his sister, Annie's mother, Mr. Vreeden made a last will and testament naming his niece, Annie, as the sole heir. Two weeks ago, the uncle died and after the funeral, Annie, accompanied by Paul Voldrop, went to see what her uncle had left her. That turned out to be a disappointment. Uncle Arnold had very few worldly possessions. He lived in an old, neglected rental house with secondhand furniture that was only good for the city dump. Uncle Arnold also had a bank account, but after estate taxes were paid, there was just enough money left for a few cheap dresses."

Vledder paused and looked at his partner.

"But here comes the interesting part. In the attic of the house, they, Annie and Paul, found a chest, a heavy antique chest with an enormous padlock of an ancient date and ironwork that looked to be just as old. They managed to break open the chest and found it filled with old prints, yellowed papers, and a small book with a leather cover."

DeKok closed his eyes as he listened to Vledder.

"It was a book about the Miracle of Amsterdam, illustrated with woodcuts by Jacob Cornelisz van Oostsaanen in 1550 and published on behalf of the Chapel Masters of the Holy City, later the New Front Fort Canal Chapel, which is built on the spot where in 1345 the miracle of the unburned Eucharist had taken place."

DeKok rubbed the back of his neck.

"Annie Scheepstra felt that the little book was worth money. The question: How much?"

Vledder waved at his screen.

"She knew that Bad Bertus dabbled in antiques and art. Much against Paul's wishes, she put the little book in her purse, traveled to Amsterdam with it, and presumably showed it to Bertus. The rest is speculation."

DeKok grinned.

"I heard what Paul Voldrop said. He thinks that Bertus probably said that the book wasn't worth a lot, but that he would let her know if he had a buyer."

"Yes, and after that he killed her, or had her killed, to obtain the book."

"Because the book was worth a fortune, according to Voldrop."

Vledder leaned back in his chair.

"Voila," he said, "a murder and a motive."

DeKok stood up and snorted.

"But without a corpse."

Outwardly unruffled, both hands in his pants pockets, DeKok ambled the next day across the sun-drenched Damrak. With an almost childish pleasure he looked at the many flags waving gaily against the stark blue sky above the docked tour boats.

In silent admiration he stopped and eyed a young woman whose well-formed and lightly clad body swayed past him. As he looked after her he saw the elegant and recently cleaned façade of Central Station. Amsterdam, he thought to himself, not for the first time, is a beautiful city. But then he reminded himself that there were a lot of people in Amsterdam who only saw it as a place to make easy money.

He glanced at the large clock in front of Central Station. It was almost eleven in the morning. After a long and tiring day, he had rewarded himself by sleeping late. A good breakfast and a long walk with his faithful dog had revived his spirits. He was ready to continue his so-called fight against crime.

He shrugged and walked through Old Bridge Alley to Warmoes Street.

As he entered the station house, the watch commander beckoned him with a crooked finger. DeKok approached the desk.

"Good morning," he said cheerfully.

The watch commander gave him a somber look and pointed at the ceiling.

There's a riot upstairs," he said.

"A riot?"

Kusters nodded.

"Vledder had to ask for assistance from another precinct," he said with distaste, "just to get that guy here. Another precinct, I tell you."

"What guy?"

Kusters turned and grabbed his logbook.

"One Richard Netherwood. He made such a racket that the entire Slotervaart Hospital was in an uproar." He grimaced. "There was a lot of consternation. Panic almost...screaming nurses, crying patients. It took about half a dozen cops to remove the guy from the premises."

The old inspector looked puzzled.

"When was this?"

"This morning."

DeKok shook his head.

"What was Vledder doing in that hospital so early? It's not in our precinct."

Kusters waved an arm in the air.

"He was there, together with Richard Netherwood. As I understand it, that guy was a witness and he was to point out certain people. Vledder said that it was your idea."

DeKok slapped both hands against his forehead. Then he shook his head, turned around, and stormed up the stairs.

Vledder, his head supported by both hands, was a picture of defeat. There was a scratch over his left eye, a few red streaks on his neck, and the collar of his jacket was torn down to the lapels. DeKok threw his old hat in the direction of the peg without looking to see if he had scored or if the hat, as usual, hit the floor. He sat down across from Vledder.

"So, what have you been up to?"

There was a hint of condemnation in his voice.

The young inspector made a tired gesture in the direction of a large yellow envelope on his desk.

"This morning I received the duty roster of Slotervaart Hospital. It was waiting on my desk. When I looked over the schedules, I noticed that today the same people are on duty that were on duty on the day Rosalind allegedly disappeared." He paused and spread both hands in an apologetic gesture. "Therefore it seemed an appropriate time to execute the reenactment you had proposed."

DeKok shook his head with the same disapproving look as before.

"Could you not have waited for me?"

Vledder looked surprised.

"But why? You said you'd be late today, and I didn't want to waste time."

DeKok sighed.

"So you were precipitous...again."

"Yes."

"So, how did you proceed?"

Vledder pointed at the telephone on his desk.

"First I asked the director, Dr. Bemmel, if he agreed, if it would not be a disruption for me to conduct a reenactment this morning. He had no objections and said he would instruct the personnel to cooperate. After that I went to Church Street and picked up Richard Netherwood."

DeKok nodded his understanding.

"Did you tell him what it was all about?"

"Of course."

"So what went wrong?"

Vledder reacted sharply.

"Nothing went wrong, not at first. Dr. Lesterhuis had arranged everything perfectly. He—"

DeKok interrupted.

"Dr. Lesterhuis, the neurologist?"

Vledder nodded.

"I found him to be a friendly, understanding man. Very sympathetic. The director had asked him to make sure that the entire staff would be available. He was determined to do anything in his power to dispel any doubt about the hospital's name and reputation."

DeKok looked up.

"Who said that?"

"Dr. Lesterhuis. He was very cooperative, as if he had a personal stake in the proceedings. In a perfectly organized fashion, the entire staff paraded through the lobby."

"The entire staff? There must have been hundreds."

"That's what I thought, but Dr. Lesterhuis, after hearing what it was all about, decided that it would be enough if just the lobby staff and the neurology staff walked by. I agreed."

DeKok gestured impatiently.

"So what went wrong?"

Vledder sighed deeply.

"When the procession was over and Dr. Lesterhuis said there were no other employees who could have been near or in the lobby at that time, I looked at Richard and asked him if he had recognized the nurse who took Rosalind away. He stared into the distance and said she wasn't there and added that the man who was behind the desk that day also had not shown up."

"Then what?"

Vledder carefully touched the painful scratch over his eye.

"I smiled and suggested that maybe the people had passed by a little fast. I asked him if he had carefully studied the faces. He nodded with a sort of faraway look in his eyes and I had the impression that my words did not really penetrate. Suddenly he stood up and walked over to Lesterhuis...slowly, threateningly. He was slightly bent over, and his arms seemed to reach for the throat of the doctor. 'Where is she?' he said in a strange, hoarse tone. 'Where is my Rosie? What have you done with her?'"

DeKok looked tensely at his partner.

"Then what?"

Vledder nervously raked his hands through his hair.

"I, eh, I saw that something was going wrong," he said hesitantly. "Richard Netherwood suddenly looked insane. I stood up and placed myself between him and the doctor and tried to separate them. But the guy was unbelievably strong. Dr. Lesterhuis fled from the lobby and Richard and I rolled around on the floor. He was completely crazy, fought like a madman. People started to scream and somebody behind the desk called the police. Luckily, the boys from Slotermeer Station were there within minutes. I was at the end of my rope."

DeKok rubbed the side of his nose with a little finger and remained silent.

Vledder squirmed in his chair.

"That's the whole story," he said defensively.

DeKok gave him a long, hard look.

"What did you do with him?"

"Who? Richard?"

"Yes."

Vledder pointed across the room.

"I put him in an interrogation room for the time being, to calm him down a little."

DeKok stood up and walked away. Vledder called him back.

"The commissaris, he wants to see you."

The old sleuth closed his eyes for a moment.

"That, too?" he said. It sounded like a curse.

7

With a slow pace, DeKok ambled along the wide corridor leading to the office of the commissaris. He tapped the center panel of the oaken door with the knuckles of his right hand. When he heard "Come" from inside the office, he slowly opened the door and closed it carefully behind him. Slowly, almost hesitantly, with slumped shoulders, he stepped closer to the desk.

The gray sleuth did not feel like having a conversation with his chief. At this stage of the investigation, he had little to offer. Except that something was not right.

In an orderly country such as Holland, people did not often disappear without a trace. That was an intolerable thought. There were countries were it happened regularly, but the Netherlands was not such a country. And if he, DeKok, had anything to say about it, there would never be a point when a disappearance was a common occurrence.

His mouth formed a wry grin at this exaggeration of his own knowledge and ability. It did not really matter what he wanted. He was constrained by a system that left little room for him to right certain wrongs.

But what exactly was wrong? How could the sudden disappearance of two young women be explained? How was he to interpret the strange circumstances that accompanied the disappearances?

These thoughts ran through his mind as he watched the commissaris rise from his chair behind the desk. His narrow, aristocratic face was expressionless, yet tense.

DeKok stopped in front of the desk and looked up. Buitendam's expression was familiar, and the inspector felt a familiar, rebellious anger forming in the pit of his stomach. Steeling himself for another fight, DeKok stood up straight and stuck out his chin.

"You wanted to see me?"

The commissaris rested both fists on his desk and leaned forward.

"DeKok," he roared angrily, "what in God's name are you doing?"

The gray sleuth remained outwardly calm.

"Is God's name," he asked unctuously, "connected with law and justice?"

The commissaris looked taken aback for a moment.

"That, eh, that is to say...yes."

DeKok nodded gratefully.

"In that case, I'm indeed involved in something in God's name," he replied calmly.

Buitendam pressed his lips together, closed his eyes for a moment, and took a deep breath.

"DeKok, I'm not interested in clever, I would almost say disrespectful, answers," he said sharply. "You can save those for others. You will account to me for your behavior."

The inspector shrugged, as if the subject hardly interested him.

"Two women have disappeared."

He made it sound as if that was answer enough.

"Who says so?" Buitendam cried. He continued without waiting for an answer. "A slimy, untrustworthy pimp and a young man who clearly shows signs of being mentally unstable?" He pointed with a shaking finger. "And on that questionable basis you accuse the management of a leading hospital in Amsterdam of…of kidnapping, or whatever crimes have occurred to your stubborn brain?"

DeKok maintained an innocent look.

"I," he defended himself, "have not made a single accusation."

Buitendam bristled.

"And on the basis of those weak assumptions you manage to create a complete panic among the patients and staff of that hospital?" He took a deep breath and exploded again. "Dr. Bemmel, the director, has communicated his displeasure about the events that took place in his hospital this morning—and in my opinion, with complete justification. He has also contacted Mr. Schaap, our judge-advocate, with the request to take the investigation out of your hands."

DeKok grinned disbelievingly.

"Dr. Bemmel…I've never met the man, never spoken to him."

Commissaris Buitendam shook his head.

"I don't want to hold young Vledder responsible for what happened this morning. After all, he acted on your orders."

DeKok nodded.

"He did," he admitted. "And if he continues to do so in the future, he has the makings of an excellent policeman, maybe even a commissaris."

Buitendam ignored the remark. A blush of irritation appeared on his pale face.

"I order you to stop this investigation immediately. You will understand that I want, at all costs, to avoid incidents such as what happened in the hospital. In addition, Dr. Bemmel has obtained permission from the secretary for health, education, and welfare to refuse any further cooperation regarding the alleged disappearance of those two women." The commissaris sat down and sighed deeply and picked up a form from his desk. "I have here your request for leave during Sail Amsterdam...the reason why I assigned the campaign against pickpockets to someone else." He looked up with a gleam of triumph in his eyes. "Your leave is granted—effective now."

DeKok looked at the form. It seemed to grow in the hands of the commissaris. Suddenly, with lightning speed that one would not expect from him, the old inspector grabbed the form from the hands of the commissaris and tore it into small pieces. He deliberately allowed the pieces to fall onto the floor and the desk. There was a recalcitrant look on his face.

"No leave," he hissed.

Buitendam flew out of his chair. His eyes shot sparks. His face was red down to his neck and his lips quivered in anger. He pointed to the door.

"OUT!"

Vledder gauged the expression of his partner when he returned to the detective room.

"Same thing again?" he asked, worried.

"What do you mean?"

"A quarrel."

DeKok sank with a sigh into his chair and leaned back.

"Worse. I've been prohibited from continuing the investigation of the vanished women." He grinned sadly. "He wanted to send me on leave at once, but I tore up the request form in front of his eyes."

Vledder looked surprised.

"But surely that is impossible."

"No, it was just paper."

"Don't joke, that's not what I meant."

"Then what is impossible?"

"Stopping the investigation."

DeKok made a helpless gesture.

"Commissaris Buitendam is a frightened man. He's always been scared, as long as I've known him. It's not that he's physically afraid, but as soon as some authority points at him, he retreats. Dr. Bemmel made a complaint to the commissaris. He has also contacted the judge-advocate, and to top it all he managed to get permission from the secretary of HEW to withdraw the hospital's active participation in the case."

Vledder shrugged.

"Therefore all the turmoil?"

"Yes, about what happened this morning."

The young inspector looked chastened.

"It's all my fault. As usual, I ran ahead of the facts,

didn't think it through, jumped to conclusions. I should have waited for you."

DeKok shook his head.

"Richard's reaction could not have been foreseen," he said resignedly. "You can, as a police officer, build a certain safety margin, but the behavior of people is, and will always be, unpredictable."

Vledder gave him a grateful look.

"That's why I did not expect it," he apologized. "The reenactment in the hospital went perfectly. It would have held up in court. When the parade had passed by, I felt relieved. I was truly glad that Richard had not recognized anyone."

DeKok gave him a hard look.

"Glad...why?"

Vledder smiled.

"I told you from the start that I didn't believe the hospital had anything to do with the disappearance of those women. The fact that our witness, Richard, did not recognize anyone was the confirmation of my theory."

The old man looked pensive.

"Did you show any of the relief you felt?"

"What do you mean?"

DeKok grinned.

"Perhaps there was someone nearby who did not share your relief."

"I don't understand you."

DeKok waved the question away. He rested his elbows on the desk and cupped his head in his hands. Suddenly he leaned forward and gave his partner a searching look.

"You've always been in contact with Dr. Bemmel?"

Vledder shrugged.

"Always?…no, twice."

DeKok nodded.

"The first time was when he made that macabre joke about a forgotten corpse in the morgue and when he said that Richard Netherwood was a paranoid young man who suffered from hallucinations."

"Exactly."

"And the second time?"

Vledder pointed at the telephone on his desk.

"That was this morning, as a result of the duty roster that had been delivered. I asked if I could stage a reenactment in the lobby, and I emphasized that I wanted to see all the personnel."

"But that proved to be impractical. A hospital has hundreds of employees on each shift."

"Yes, that's why I went along with Dr. Lesterhuis's suggestion."

DeKok rubbed his nose with a little finger.

"And both times," he formulated carefully, "when you contacted Dr. Bemmel, it was in connection with the disappearance of Rosalind Evertsoord?"

"Yes."

DeKok pointed an index finger in the direction of his partner.

"You did not mention the disappearance of Annie Scheepstra at any time?"

"No."

"Nor in the hospital, while you were talking to Dr. Lesterhuis?"

Vledder shook his head.

"It never came up."

DeKok rubbed his chin, a faraway look in his eyes.

"Then how," he said slowly, "could Bemmel ask the secretary to stop the investigation for both women? And how come the secretary agreed and promised him that he no longer had to cooperate?"

Vledder's mouth fell open.

"Is it true?" he panted. "Was there discussion of both women?"

DeKok nodded with emphasis.

"Absolutely."

The young man swallowed.

"But that means that…it means that Bemmel also knows about Annie Scheepstra's disappearance."

DeKok's expression hardened.

"Exactly. The question is how. Bad Bertus never reported her disappearance, except to us and we did not discuss it. So how did Bemmel gain that knowledge?"

With mixed feelings, DeKok looked down. Richard Netherwood sat behind the table, his head resting on his crossed forearms. He wore the same jacket of rough tweed as before…how long ago it seemed when he had first come to report the disappearance of his Rosie.

The young man seemed asleep and did not notice DeKok's entrance into the small interrogation room. The old inspector tapped him on the shoulder. With a scared look, Richard slowly straightened up. He raked his fingers through his hair.

"Oh," he murmured, "it's you."

DeKok smiled.

"Yes, it's me," he said simply.

Richard shook a shiver from his body.

"Where were you this morning?"

DeKok pushed a chair closer to the table and sat down.

"You mean while you were at the hospital?"

Richard nodded.

"I missed you."

DeKok shrugged.

"It was rather late last night when I finally got home," he apologized. "Almost three o'clock. So I thought I'd sleep in."

Richard Netherwood shook his head in disapproval.

"You should never have left that situation in the hospital in the hands of that young man."

"You mean my colleague Vledder?"

"Yes, the same young man who was with you when I reported the disappearance of Rosie. Perhaps he is a competent inspector. I wouldn't know. But in the hospital this morning he showed little insight."

DeKok moved in his chair.

"Little insight? In what way?"

Richard Netherwood waved emotionally.

"The show."

"What show?"

"The show," he repeated with emphasis. "The farce, the revue, the parade—a costumed ball in work clothes. The personnel of the Slotervaart Hospital, neatly washed, shaved, polished, and combed. Everyone enjoyed it... including your colleague and that Dr. Lesterhuis—and I looked like an idiot!"

8

DeKok remained silent while Richard vented. He understood the young man's anger, his disappointment. After a
while he took Rosalind's photo from an inside pocket and
placed it on the table in front of him. For a long time he
looked at the laughing face of the pretty young woman,
the short blond hair, the dimpled cheeks.

Slowly he turned the picture around and pushed it in
Richard's direction.

"Your Rosie."

Richard Netherwood nodded. The tension disappeared from his face. A sad smile curled his lips.

"My Rosie."

There was genuine sorrow in his voice.

"Did you love her?"

"Yes."

"And what about her?"

The young man hesitated for a moment.

"I thought she loved me."

DeKok listened to the tone.

"But why did you both stay in your own apartments?
I mean, why did you not live together...why didn't you
marry?"

Richard looked at the photo.

"She didn't want that. As long as basketball was in her life, she did not want to marry. 'I can't do that to you,' she always said. 'You'd only have half of me, and that's no basis for marriage.' She was very conscientious about that."

DeKok nodded.

"I take it that sport was often the subject of your conversation. How long did Rosie plan to compete?"

Richard smiled.

"For the time being I was in second place."

"No chance of moving up?"

The young man shrugged.

"I never had any illusions about that. When I saw the dedication that Rosie gave to her sport, I realized again and again how she valued her achievements. She always played with total abandon and enthusiasm. I admired that. She had just returned with her team from an exhibition tour through Central Africa. Very successful. There were plans for an extended trip to the Far East."

DeKok pulled out his lower lip and let it plop back. He repeated the annoying gesture several times.

"So there was no wedding in the future?"

Richard's face clouded over. Slowly he stretched out a hand to the photo and pushed it back toward DeKok.

"Rosie will never be my bride."

DeKok feigned surprise.

"Why not?"

Richard swallowed.

"She's dead."

DeKok narrowed his eyes.

"How do you know that?"

The young man shook his head.

"It's not a matter of knowing, nothing to do with facts. It's a matter of feeling." He tapped his chest with the tips of his fingers. "Here, within me, I feel it: Rosie is no longer alive."

DeKok leaned his head to one side.

"As a police officer I can only deal with facts. That's my profession—facts, evidence, proof. But just a feeling, no matter how strong or how essential, no, it doesn't help me at all."

"I'm sorry."

DeKok looked at the young man for a long time. Although he sincerely tried to feel sympathetic toward him, he did not succeed. There was something in his behavior that bothered DeKok, something that awoke a sort of revulsion.

"Feelings," he said finally, irked, "sometimes have a history. We draw conclusions and because they are irrational, not supported by facts, we call them *feelings*."

Richard sighed.

"If Rosie was alive, she would have contacted me," he said bitterly. "She would have told me what was the matter...why she couldn't come back...why she left me sitting in that miserable hospital."

"Even if there was another man involved?"

It sounded sharper than he intended.

Richard gave him a pitying smile.

"You didn't know Rosie," he said condescendingly. "Otherwise you would never have asked that question. I told you, she was very conscientious. If another man had come into her life, she would have told me. She would have said that she no longer loved me and then she would have tried to explain why."

With a sigh, DeKok leaned back in his chair. He had the feeling that the barrier behind which Richard hid was impenetrable.

"Yesterday we found her car," he said carelessly.

For a moment the young man narrowed his eyes.

"Where?"

"At the bottom of the North-Holland Canal, at a place where barges sometimes load and unload cargo."

"Then it was in Old Purmerend."

"Yes."

"And Rosie was no longer in her car?"

"No."

Richard smiled.

"I had not expected that."

DeKok gave him a penetrating look.

"Why not?"

The young man shook his head.

"Rosie never went to the old part of Purmerend. If she came from Amsterdam, she would turn off at Gores Lane. It's the shortest way to her apartment." He paused and rubbed the back of his neck. "No matter what conclusions you want to draw from finding her car, Rosie did not drown in the North-Holland Canal."

"You're sure of that?"

Richard Netherwood nodded. His face was pale and the corners of his mouth quivered.

"She wore that mask earlier."

"What mask?"

"The mask of death."

Vledder took both hands from the wheel and shook his fists.

"That guy is nuts. I've said it before. Not just crazy, but very dangerous. We should have him examined by a psychiatrist. If a doctor decides that Richard Netherwood is indeed paranoid and suffers from hallucinations, our entire case is out the window."

DeKok corrected him.

"As you know very well, that's impossible. The law does not allow psychiatric evaluations of witnesses. Besides, you forget a few things."

"Such as?"

"Two completely vanished women…and a car in the North-Holland Canal."

Vledder shook his head angrily.

"We have to redirect our investigation. Slotervaart Hospital is no longer a factor." He glanced at his partner. "Richard wants us to concentrate on the hospital. That is why he started such a riot this morning. The failed investigation did not fit into his strategy."

"And what is his strategy?" demanded DeKok.

Vledder rhythmically slapped the dashboard with a flat hand.

"To divert attention from himself. That's why he pooh-poohed the finding of the car in the canal. He wants us to find that aspect less important."

DeKok nodded to himself.

"By which you infer that it really is very important."

"Precisely."

"And the mask of death?"

The young inspector grinned.

"DeKok," he exclaimed dramatically, "where is your insight, your ability to faultlessly analyze all aspects of a crime?"

The gray sleuth looked amused.

"I don't think I understand you."

Vledder snorted.

"What sort of mask is that?"

DeKok gestured vaguely.

"According to Richard, something had definitely changed his Rosie. He immediately noticed it that morning when she picked him up in her car. She looked a bit gray and the skin of her face looked unusually taut...as if she had undergone an exaggerated face-lift."

Vledder lifted his chin.

"And what does that indicate?"

DeKok shrugged.

"Some sort of illness."

Vledder looked triumphant.

"And where does an illness lead us?"

"To a hospital."

In his enthusiasm, the young inspector slapped the steering wheel and spread wide both arms.

"Voila, and then we're right back where Richard Netherwood wants us."

DeKok nodded agreement.

"Slotervaart Hospital."

Vledder started the VW and they pulled out of the
parking space where they had finished their discussion.
DeKok had not wanted to discuss the case in the station house.

"We're still going to Purmerend?" asked Vledder.

"Yes."

For a while they drove on in silence. DeKok straightened up in his seat and looked around. A bright sun
drenched the landscape in light. To the left were ships and
yachts sailing in the canal, and to the right were green
fields dotted with black-and-white cows.

The old inspector loved the North-Holland landscape
and was firmly decided that he would retire somewhere
in the north. He regretted that small towns such as Purmerend and Hoorn were slowly but surely becoming
bedroom communities for Amsterdam. He would have
to go farther north, perhaps even past Alkmaar, to find
the old, intimate towns.

Suddenly he realized that this was now the third time
that he was on his way to Purmerend in connection with
the mysterious case. Despite Vledder's scoffing, he found it
remarkable that the two vanished women both came from
Purmerend and that both had apparently been referred to
Slotervaart Hospital by a doctor in Purmerend.

But that was the end of their similarities. Rosalind
Evertsoord was an independent, conscientious, and
athletic woman with a strong competitive drive; Annie
Scheepstra was a somewhat laconic, careless girl of questionable morals who did not take life too seriously.

And there was another difference that got the gray
sleuth thinking. Both women had complained about

being listless and weary before they went to see the doctor. But Richard was of the opinion that his Rosie wore a mask of death, while Paul Voldrop remembered that he was pressed to keep up with Annie…whatever that meant.

DeKok slapped his forehead. It was about time that his brain took an active part—only two days until Sail Amsterdam and he did not want to miss it again. Last time he had missed it because he had been involved in the investigation of a murder, supposedly committed by the daughter of his friend Handy Henkie, the ex-burglar.

Vledder interrupted his train of thought.

"Are you planning to ignore the prohibition of the commissaris?"

"What prohibition?"

Vledder looked surprised.

"I thought you were prohibited from handling this case."

DeKok grinned.

"For that antipickpocket team he's found someone else already. He won't pick me for that job now. But for the time being I'm staying out of his sight. I think that's best."

Vledder laughed.

"But what if he comes up with another unpleasant job for you?"

DeKok shook his head.

"His prohibition doesn't impress me," he said calmly. "And nobody can forbid me from accidentally making some discoveries."

"Such as?"

DeKok searched one of his pockets, produced a set of keys, and showed them to Vledder.

"This means free access to Rosalind's apartment."

"How did you get those?"

DeKok smiled.

"Freely given by Richard Netherwood. I asked him if he had a key to Rosie's apartment and if he had been there after she disappeared. He asked why he should and then he took the keys out of his pocket and tossed them to me."

Vledder nodded.

"At least it won't be breaking and entering. That'll be a change. What do you expect to find in her apartment?"

DeKok put the keys back in his pocket.

"Actually, I've no idea. We'll just look around. Perhaps there will be indications that Rosie was still alive after she went to the hospital."

"That would be nice. But how would you recognize such an indication?"

DeKok made a dismissive gesture.

"Papers, letters, a suicide note...who knows."

Vledder narrowed his eyes but did not take them off the road.

"A suicide note?" he questioned. "Did she plan suicide?"

DeKok shrugged.

"Surely you're not going to maintain that Rosalind Evertsoord committed suicide?"

DeKok had a stubborn look on his face.

"As long as we're groping completely in the dark, everything remains a possibility."

Vledder grinned.

"But you don't go to a hospital if you plan to commit suicide."

DeKok rubbed his face.

"But afterward?"

Vledder looked stunned.

"Of course," he almost stuttered, "that's possible. Rosie heard in the hospital that she had an incurable disease and decided on suicide...then drove her car into the canal."

9

Vledder drove into the parking lot. He parked the junked-up police car out of sight under some overhanging bushes. Then he turned the key and got out of the car. DeKok followed his example, though a bit more laboriously. After a drive of some distance in the old Bug, he always felt as if his crooked bones would never straighten out. That's why within the city he often preferred to walk or take a streetcar. But this time it was not too bad. After a few seconds of strenuous stretching, he felt revived.

Both inspectors looked up. The apartment building towered above the trees. The gaily decorated balconies gave the building a festive look.

Vledder pointed.

"If we find evidence that Rosalind was still alive after her visit to the hospital, then we can offer our apologies to Bemmel and his staff." He sighed deeply. "It would be a load off my mind."

DeKok glanced at him with a puzzled look.

"Why is that?"

The young inspector raised a finger.

"First, because I never really believed in the hospital's involvement, and second," he raised a second finger, "if it appears that Rosalind did not commit suicide, then we can finally search for some evidence against Richard Netherwood."

DeKok listened carefully to the tone of voice.

"So all of a sudden you no longer believe in suicide?"

Vledder shook his head.

"I thought about it for a while. You see, if the hospital had diagnosed a serious disease or illness, they would have told us that and the entire event this morning would have been superfluous. But that story of Richard Netherwood's is one hundred percent fantasy: Rosie has never been to Slotervaart Hospital. Therefore it's clear as glass that Richard has deliberately tried to lead us down the wrong path."

He paused and bit his lower lip, deep in thought.

"I have an idea that Richard arranged for Rosie's car to wind up in the water and only after that did he come to us with the story about the hospital."

The old inspector did not react. He slammed shut the door of the car and ambled away in the direction of the building. Rather than think about Vledder's remarks, he worried why he had not sooner taken a look in Rosie's apartment.

He intensely disliked the mysterious disappearance of people. He preferred to start his investigations with an honest-to-goodness corpse—a corpse with clear signs of murder, like a strangled throat, a dented skull, recognizable bullet holes. In his long career he had never been able to immediately bring all his faculties to bear when there was no corpse. The looming possibility that the presumed deceased would suddenly appear alive and well made him unsure at the beginning of a case.

Vledder walked next to him.

"I've asked the water police if they would dredge."

"Where?"

"In the North-Holland Canal. Where else?"

DeKok glanced aside.

"And do you expect any results?"

"Of course I expect results. Otherwise I would not have asked. Murder or suicide, her body must be found."

"Even if she wasn't in the car?"

"What do you mean?"

DeKok nodded calmly.

"That's possible, isn't it? It is not too far-fetched to theorize that just the car was rolled into the water."

Vledder swallowed.

"But in that case, where is she?"

DeKok grinned broadly.

"Yes, if we knew that, we would have already solved the riddle of her disappearance."

Vledder remained silent.

They entered the spacious lobby of the apartment building. It was pleasantly cool. To the right, against the wall, stood a neglected, green algae–covered aquarium.

To the left was a metal panel with black push buttons and names.

The gray sleuth took a look at the closed door of the super's office and then walked over to the panel. His finger slid toward number 705. He looked at Vledder with a hint of surprise.

"It's gone."

"What?"

"The plate...the nameplate next to the button for her apartment. Richard Netherwood confirmed that as her apartment." He put his hand in his pocket and drew out the keys. "See, the label on the keys also indicates 705."

Vledder shrugged.

"Is this the right building?"

"Yes."

"Maybe Rosie never had a nameplate."

DeKok looked at the remnants of glue and dropped the subject. He walked over to the heavy glass door at the end of the lobby. One of the keys fit the door and he stepped through, followed by Vledder. They found themselves in a tiled hallway lined with elevator doors. It looked clean and well cared for.

They entered an elevator and DeKok pushed the button for the seventh floor. Silently the elevator rose and stopped. The doors opened and the two men stepped into a long corridor. The apartment they were looking for was three doors down from the elevator.

DeKok pointed at some slight damage on the wall underneath the bell.

"Here, too, her nameplate has been removed," he whispered.

He leaned forward and slid the second key into the lock. They both felt the tension rise. Carefully, slowly, DeKok turned the handle and pushed open the door.

Shocked, he looked into the apartment.

Vledder panted behind him, "The apartment is empty!"

In silence, with somber faces, they drove back to Amsterdam. Discovering that Rosalind's apartment had been completely stripped was an unpleasant surprise that intensified their already bad mood. Their investigation seemed to be at a dead end.

Vledder was the first to break the silence.

"This is the last time," he growled. "From now on we stay in our own precinct. I'm not going back to that cursed town, that, eh, that Purmerend." He managed to make the name of the town sound like an insult.

The gray sleuth shifted in the uncomfortable seat.

"Completely...and I mean completely stripped of everything. Not a chair, a table, the carpeting was lifted, and even the wallpaper had been stripped from the walls."

Vledder sighed deeply.

"Why?"

DeKok made an exasperated gesture.

"No idea," he said. "What did the super tell you?"

Vledder nodded.

"Nice man, friendly, but he didn't know anything either. Three days ago, while he and his wife were at the theater, it seems a van showed up. Within an hour everything had been removed from the apartment and loaded up. The van drove away."

DeKok grimaced.

"Three days ago...that was the day she disappeared."

"Exactly."

"How did he know?"

"What?"

"About the van."

"Some of the other tenants told him. That was a bit later, after he discovered that number 705 was no longer occupied and he asked around."

DeKok nodded his understanding.

"Any indications—name on the van, address, license plate?"

Vledder shook his head.

"Nothing, absolutely nothing. The only thing that some of the neighbors seemed to have noticed was that the movers, if that was who they were, kept three of the six elevators in constant use. They did not use the freight elevator. Besides, the tenants hardly know each other. There are two hundred and forty apartments in the building, twenty-four to a floor. And most of the residents are commuters to Amsterdam. They leave early in the morning and come back late at night. Nobody finds it strange if somebody moves in or out."

"Are there new tenants for the apartment?"

"No."

DeKok rubbed the back of his neck.

"It would be worth something," he mused, "if we knew who gave the order for the removal."

Vledder's face became less somber.

"Perhaps she did that herself."

"Rosie?" He sounded skeptical.

"Of course," said Vledder. "I figure it's another possibility that Rosie wanted to break off her relationship with Richard. Well, she did it in a meticulous manner—completely and with finality. And just to make sure that any future contact would be almost impossible, she drove her car into the canal. After that she left...destination unknown."

DeKok pulled his nose.

"And you find that a workable theory?" he asked, doubt in his voice.

Vledder nodded.

"Yes."

DeKok shook his head.

"I don't."

The young man briefly glanced aside.

"But there is something to be said for my theory," he said defensively. "I had a careful look around, before and after I talked to the super. There are absolutely no signs of breaking and entering, no forced entry. The movers had keys to her apartment."

DeKok looked out the window.

"She gave them the keys?"

Vledder slapped the steering wheel with one hand.

"Who else?" he demanded.

DeKok did not answer. He slid down in the seat and pushed his little hat over his eyes. For a long time they drove on in silence. Suddenly DeKok sat up.

"Did you smell anything peculiar in that apartment?"

"What?" asked Vledder, puzzled.

"Did you smell anything in her apartment?" repeated DeKok impatiently.

"No, you?"

DeKok nodded slowly.

"An odor...almost undetectable, but it clung to the walls."

"What kind of odor?"

DeKok sank back in the seat.

"As if somebody had disinfected the apartment."

Vledder entered the tunnel underneath the Ij and took Prince Henry Quay to the Damrak. Much to DeKok's surprise, he drove on until he arrived at recently restored Willem's Gate. He parked the car and shut off the engine.

"What are you doing?"

The young man looked at his watch.

"I'm waiting until five o'clock."

"Why?"

Vledder grinned.

"I don't want you to run into the commissaris at the station house...who knows what would happen." He turned toward DeKok. "And in a way it's also self-preservation. I can't imagine what would happen if I had to handle the case by myself."

The old man smiled. The sudden frankness of his younger colleague moved him deeply. He placed a hand on Vledder's shoulder.

"I would have helped you on the sly."

Vledder nodded to himself.

"I believe that. But I'd rather have you with me openly. You see things that I don't." He smiled. "And you smell smells that completely pass me by."

DeKok did not react. He opened the window on the passenger side and looked dreamily at the rush-hour traffic that crawled around Haarlem Square. Amsterdam, he thought, a world-class city, built for a barge, a wheelbarrow, and a handcart.

Vledder looked at his watch.

"It's almost five thirty," he said. "I'm sure the commissaris has left by now." Vledder started the engine and entered the fray of the traffic with his ramshackle vehicle. It took almost half an hour to get to the station house. He drove around the side and parked behind the building. Through Old Bridge Alley they ambled toward the entrance of the police station.

As they entered the lobby, Jan Kusters looked up from his logbook.

"Somebody is waiting for you upstairs," he announced.

DeKok approached the desk.

"Again?" he growled. "I can't leave for a moment without somebody showing up for me."

Kusters grinned.

"I can't help it that you're so popular," he joked.

DeKok ignored the remark.

"Who is it?"

"Bad Bertus."

"Bad Bertus?" repeated DeKok, a hint of suspicion in his voice.

The watch commander nodded.

"I told him that I had no idea when you would be back…if you would be back, but he refused to leave. He said he'd wait until you got here."

DeKok looked disbelieving.

"So, what's his problem?"

Jan Kusters looked serious.

"He says he's received death threats."

10

DeKok looked at his visitor as he sank down in the chair behind his desk.

"Really," his tone was skeptical, "I would never have believed that you would lower yourself to the point where you voluntarily come to the station."

Bertus listened to the mocking tone. He unbuttoned his jacket and sat down across from DeKok.

"Usually I can do very well without you," he said solemnly. "You know that as well as I do. I've always been able to take care of myself. But I want to be done with the harassment."

"What harassment?"

Bertus made an annoyed gesture.

"Obnoxious, strange phone calls with veiled threats. 'Dirty old man, you'd better make your last will and testament…get your grave ready and have your insurance papers in order…you'll be dead before you know it.'"

"Not very friendly."

Bad Bertus nodded agreement.

"I'm just tired of answering the phone. Of course, I could go to the phone company and get an unlisted number. But I refuse to do that. But if this continues…" He did not complete the sentence. "This morning some bastard actually asked me what I had done with the corpse."

DeKok pounced.

"What corpse?"

Bertus moved in his chair.

"Annie's corpse." The pimp raised his bright blue eyes to look DeKok full in the face. "That's what this is all about—Annie, Annie Scheepstra. That guy—you know, the one she shacked up with in Purmerend—thinks that I killed her."

"And that's not so?"

Bad Bertus arched his back and with a theatrical gesture raised his right hand in the air.

"I have had nothing to do with the disappearance of that child, I swear to God."

DeKok regarded him coolly.

"Do you believe in God?"

"Well, now, eh, no."

"Then why do you swear?"

Bad Bertus made a desperate gesture.

"Because it's the truth," he offered. "Things happened exactly as I told you. I took her to the hospital and that was it. I mean, I never saw her again after that. I told that guy the same thing, but he won't believe me. He threatened to send a couple of guys from his boxing club after me. I think he also uses those boys to call and threaten me. There are always different voices." With a wild gesture he took his wallet from a pocket and held it up high. "If I wave this around here in the neighborhood, I'll have enough help in no time at all to knock him and his boxing club into the next world. But I don't want that.

I'm a peaceful man, I don't like force, never did."

DeKok chewed his lower lip.

"Why," he asked carefully, "does that guy think you killed Annie?"

Drops of sweat beaded Bertus's forehead. He grinned, embarrassed.

"Because of a little book…a little old book."

DeKok nodded calmly.

"A book about the Miracle of Amsterdam, illustrated with woodcuts by Jacob Cornelisz van Oostsaanen, published in 1550?"

Bad Bertus did not answer at once. A weary look appeared in his blue eyes.

"He's been to see you?"

"Who?"

"That guy Paul."

DeKok grinned.

"He claims that you stole the book from Annie."

Bad Bertus produced a big handkerchief and wiped the sweat off his forehead.

"That's crazy," he said angrily. "Has he filed a complaint?"

"Not officially."

The pimp leaned closer.

"Annie," he said patiently, "came to see me and showed me the book. She said she had found it in some antique chest that she had inherited from her uncle. The uncle was some sort of director of a Christian community, here in Amsterdam." He paused and leaned back in his chair. Again he wiped his forehead. "I've been dabbling in antiques for years. Not always for the money. It's more a kind of hobby of mine. I admit, I was interested in the book. It looked good. I've built some relationships over the years...people I sold things to. I promised her I'd look for a buyer."

"And what did Annie say?"

Bertus made a nonchalant gesture.

"She thought that was a good idea, and she said that she'd wait to hear from me."

"And did you find a buyer?"

The pimp shook his head.

"It's not all that easy, not as easy as it used to be. Back in the day you could always sell something. But people no longer trust each other. There's so much kitsch, fakes, and frauds in the market. People—"

DeKok interrupted.

"What went wrong?"

Bertus looked puzzled.

"What do you mean?"

DeKok reacted with irritation. He pointed an accusing finger at the man.

"Listen, Bertus," he said angrily, "if that antique transaction had been conducted peacefully, then Annie would probably not have disappeared and you wouldn't be here complaining."

Bertus again took out his handkerchief.

"It's all because of that guy."

"How?"

"He demanded two million."

DeKok looked surprised.

"Two million?"

"For that miracle book."

"And Annie knew about that?"

Bad Bertus looked unsure.

"I think so. The book belonged to her. She must have discussed it with that guy. Everybody thinks I'm stinking rich."

"When was the first time two million guilders was mentioned?"

Bertus made a helpless gesture.

"I had it less than a week. I didn't have time to have it appraised."

DeKok rubbed his nose with a little finger.

"Did you pay the two million?" he asked carelessly.

The pimp grinned.

"You must think I'm crazy. I told him he'd have to try to get two million for it on his own. Then I returned the book to Annie."

"When was that?"

"The morning I took her to the hospital."

After Bertus had left, DeKok started to pace up and down the room. A slight anger was rising in him as he obsessed over the mystery of the vanished women. The fact that after days of investigation he had made no progress irritated him. He suddenly stopped in front of Vledder's desk.

"It doesn't fit," he said, visibly upset. "There's something wrong." He waved his arms around. "With Annie's cooperation, Paul Voldrop demands a couple million guilders for that little book. The conversations regarding that must have been anything but friendly. Yet when

Annie has to go to the hospital in Amsterdam, she asks Bertus to accompany her." He shook his head. "People don't behave like that."

The young inspector grinned.

"And Paul Voldrop—after Annie's disappearance—becomes angry and starts making threats."

DeKok nodded. Vledder continued.

"And he presumes that Bertus has killed her to gain possession of the book." He raised a finger in the air. "His suspicions are raised even more after he inquires at Slotervaart Hospital, when he learns that she was never there." The young inspector gave his partner a hopeful look. "What do you think, should we arrest him?"

"Who?"

"Bad Bertus."

"For what?"

"Murder, the murder of Annie Scheepstra."

DeKok lowered his chin to his chest.

"He'll laugh at us, and with reason. Before we even get him to the station, there will be half a dozen lawyers waiting for us." He shook his head. "We don't have a shred of evidence…not even a body."

DeKok went over to his desk and sat down behind it. He felt the anger within him diminish and he regained a measure of composure. Thoughtfully, he looked at Vledder.

"Bertus," he said, "says that he took Annie to the hospital by taxi. It should be possible to find out what taxi took them there. Cabs keep logs of their trips, and maybe the driver will remember something about that trip."

Vledder was annoyed.

"That's wasted time. Bertus lied. That trip never existed."

DeKok was unmoved.

"Humor me," he said.

Suddenly the telephone on DeKok's desk rang. As usual, DeKok ignored it. Vledder leaned over and lifted the receiver. Silently he made a few notes. Then he thanked the caller and hung up.

"Who was that?" asked DeKok.

"The police, eh, Slotermeer Station."

"And?"

"Another two young women have disappeared."

"Where?"

Vledder shook his head and closed his eyes.

"In Slotervaart Hospital."

11

For a long time Inspector DeKok stared into the distance, concentrating. The news that again two young women had disappeared in Slotervaart Hospital had not shocked him as much as he had expected. In fact, in the back of his mind he had expected some such happening. He was trying to see the connection. There had to be a relationship between the women, a common denominator.

He looked at Vledder, who seemed depressed.

"What's the matter?"

The young inspector shook his head.

"It's just plain impossible," he said, trying to convince himself. "There are no criminal hospitals in Holland."

DeKok smiled.

"But there may be criminals in hospitals."

"Never!"

"Who says so?"

Vledder grinned, abashed.

"Well," he began excitedly, "as I see it, there are now four women who have mysteriously disappeared in the same hospital."

DeKok leaned his head to one side.

"As you see it?"

Vledder sighed deeply.

"Yes," he said reluctantly.

DeKok grimaced.

"It seems hard for you to admit that."

Vledder made an apologetic gesture.

"I would never have believed it." Again he shook his head. "And I still don't want to believe it. I think we'll find it's not true after all."

DeKok ignored the remark.

"What did Slotermeer Station have to say?"

Vledder snorted.

"They seemed pretty agitated. The fact that they didn't follow up on Richard's first report must have played a part. They wanted to know if you had made any progress."

"I didn't hear you say anything."

He stuck out his chin.

"I didn't think it was any of their business."

DeKok feigned disapproval.

"Do you have the names of those women?"

Vledder consulted his notes.

"Marie Antoinette Houten, a twenty-five-year-old psychology student, and Charlotte Sloot, a twenty-three-year-old daughter of an Amsterdam bar owner. No known profession or school affiliation."

"Relationship to each other...family?"

Vledder shrugged.

"They didn't say and I didn't ask."

DeKok nodded to himself.

"Did they say they would start an immediate investigation? Is there a plan of action?"

"No."

DeKok stood up. He pointed at his partner.

"You go to Slotermeer Station. Use a car. Tell them that Warmoes Street Station is taking over the case. Completely. As I remember, Slotermeer has only one homicide detective assigned. Tell them that we will call him if needed." He rubbed his nose. "I don't want them to interfere, perhaps at cross-purposes. Get all the information you can and then visit the people who reported the disappearances."

"Why?"

DeKok gestured impatiently.

"I want all possible details of their relationships, family, clubs, memberships, hobbies. Mention the names of Rosalind and Annie. Observe how they react to those names."

"Then what?"

"Then you come back here."

Vledder looked up.

"What are you going to do?"

DeKok did not answer. He merely smiled. He walked away from his desk and went over to the peg where he kept his raincoat and hat.

Vledder stood up and called out, "You're not coming with me?"

The gray sleuth shook his head. He glanced at the clock on the wall, put on his raincoat, and grabbed his hat.

"I, eh, I," he said vaguely, "I'm going to visit someone."

Vledder seemed taken aback.

At the door DeKok turned around.

"Just keep one thing in mind," he called.

"What?"

"The mask of death."

When DeKok stepped outside, he wrinkled his nose as he looked at the sky. Dark clouds had drifted over Amsterdam and it began to drizzle. He pushed his hat forward and raised the collar of his coat. Despite the rain, he did not increase his slow, ambling gait. He crossed the Damrak and disappeared into a maze of streets. Eventually he reached Blue Fort Canal.

He liked this area of the old canal, despite the fact that an inept architect had made a mess of restoring some of the façades that had been bombed during the opening days of the war in 1940.

He walked on past Gentlemen's Canal and Emperor's Canal to Prince's Canal. Deep in thought, he ambled along the narrow sidewalk. It was quiet here, almost oppressively quiet. The roar of traffic had disappeared into the distance. Along the canal's edge he heard the rustling of a stray rat. He ignored it, as he ignored the rain. The many riddles surrounding the vanished women occupied his thoughts.

What could a simple inspector do when put toe to toe with a mighty hospital? Who should be called into account for the young women's disappearances? The director, other doctors, the board of directors?

What were his options? A tumultuous confrontation, such as this morning's, could not be afforded. What remained? A sudden raid? Who would give him permission? Besides, where would he look? In the morgue for leftover corpses, as Dr. Bemmel had mockingly suggested?

A big hospital, he mused, is actually an ideal place to hide someone. If necessary, the faces could be wrapped in bandages and nobody would be recognized. Grinning at the thought, DeKok entered North Market. Diagonally across from the market, behind the English Reformed Church, he stopped in front of a narrow house with a high window. In the center of the glass was a legend in elegant scroll letters: "Peter Karstens." Under that, in smaller letters, was printed "Painter, Artist."

DeKok glanced at the tower of the church and, much to his amazement, he found it to be almost eleven o'clock.

"As usual, an unchristian hour for a visit," he said to himself. But that did not prevent him from giving a yank on the brass-bell pull. He heard the clang of the bell inside the house, loud and insistent. DeKok was not worried about the noise. He had known the occupant for a long time and was familiar with his nocturnal habits.

It took about two minutes, and then the door was opened by a man with dark-blond hair, dressed in sweat-pants and a black, gleaming silk shirt. He frowned until he recognized DeKok.

"DeKok!" exclaimed the man with a mixture of surprise and delight. "My goodness, what's up? What an ungodly hour to arrest someone."

DeKok laughed.

"I'm not here to arrest you, Peter," he said pleasantly. "Just a friendly visit."

The artist hesitated for a moment. Then he performed a slight bow and spread his arms wide. It was a gracious, old-fashioned gesture, and DeKok approved thoroughly.

"Trusty henchman of capitalism," joked Peter, "enter my humble abode." It was a long-standing joke between them.

DeKok gave him a mock withering look.

"Please be careful how you express yourself. I'm not a henchman of capitalism. I'm a henchman of the law."

The artist pulled on his short Vandyke beard.

"Isn't that just about the same thing?"

DeKok shook his head and smiled. He entered, and Karstens led the way to a staircase. After passing through a short corridor at the bottom of the stairs, they stepped into a comfortable, cozy room with a low ceiling. A rough wooden table supported a set of candles, a few bottles of wine, and two crystal glasses. A painting with a cloth draped over it stood on an easel in one corner.

DeKok looked around and discovered a young woman in the shadows. He had met her several times before. She was Karstens's favorite model and, second to painting, the love of his life. She rested elegantly on a wide leather settee, her knees pulled up underneath her. She was extremely beautiful, he thought not for the first time. In the half-light of the candles she had an uncommon, ethereal beauty. Her ivory-colored skin glowed in the soft light and her mouth displayed a mysterious smile. Long, wavy black hair descended in luxurious ripples down to her naked chest. It made him dizzy. His puritanical soul was always a bit confused when confronted with such blatant sexuality.

Peter Karstens waved casually in her direction.

"Allow me to introduce you to my love, Maria."

"I know," murmured DeKok.

Slowly she came to her feet, tossed her hair back with an impatient gesture, and unashamedly displayed herself. She stepped forward with the agility of a cat and shook hands with DeKok. Her breasts bobbed pleasingly. DeKok kept his gaze on her face.

"Inspector DeKok," announced Karstens in a declarative voice, "a jewel in the crown of Amsterdam's forces of law and order."

"I know that, Pete. Do be quiet," she said huskily.

DeKok ignored the announcement and the response. He looked deep into Maria's dark eyes and noted a hint of amusement. With a slight pressure, she released his hand, walked around him, and helped him out of his coat. She hung it on a hat rack and then held out a hand. DeKok meekly gave her his hat.

"Peter never thinks of those things," she said and went back to the settee. She crossed her slender legs and pulled a wrap around her shoulders, covering her front at the same time. Suddenly, with the wrap around her, she looked as chaste as a nun, but still as beautiful.

DeKok shook his head as if to clear his vision. Then he looked at his host. Karstens, who had the untamed soul of a true artist, lived in a kind of uneasy truce with the rest of society. Perhaps that was why the man was so dear to DeKok's heart. Both men, at times, were convinced they had been born several hundred years too late.

Karstens pointed at the table.

"You'll have a glass of wine with us?"

"Still Burgundy?"

"Always, although it becomes more and more expensive. The French vintners...in the old days they pressed wine out of grapes, but now...gold."

Peter Karstens poured carefully, but generously. The light from the candle gave the wine an extra deep, rich color.

DeKok accepted the glass and tasted. The wine was indeed superb. While the liquid poured like velvet down his throat, DeKok gave Karstens a good look. He guessed that the artist had emptied more than a few glasses already. Peter seemed in a happy, excited mood. He sat down next to Maria and handed her a glass as well. She sipped delicately.

"Why are you here?" asked Karstens. "I can't imagine that such a dedicated cop would stop by just for a friendly visit."

DeKok smiled.

"I'm here as a friend...and a cop."

Peter shook his head.

"Impossible. Those are irreconcilable differences." He paused and gave DeKok a long, hard look. "If you're here as a friend, empty your glass and I'll pour again. But if you're here as a cop, as a representative of the law, tell me what's on your mind."

DeKok slowly drained his glass and then placed it on the rough wooden table. He looked resignedly at the artist.

"It's up to you if you want to pour again."

Karstens hesitated for just a few seconds. Then, in response to a hardly noticeable nudge from Maria, he stood up with a wide grin on his face. He poured with style and handed the full glass to DeKok.

"You know, DeKok," he said pensively, looking at

Maria, who gave him an approving smile, "as a cursed representative of the law, you're not all that bad."

DeKok grinned in appreciation. The full-bodied wine warmed his insides, and he would have been happy to forget all about the reason for his visit. Preferably he would have liked to pull up a chair, put his feet up, and chat away the rest of the night. But the memory of four vanished women brought him back to reality. With a sigh he replaced his glass and leaned closer.

"I appreciate your hospitality, I really do. But I'm here because of the miracle book."

Peter Karstens laughed out loud.

"Here begins," he orated in Old Dutch, "the findings of the respected and Holy Sacrament, in fire and flame miraculously remained untouched and conserved the whole—"

DeKok interrupted.

"I know it's Medieval Dutch," he said, "and it is just about as comprehensible as Medieval English. But I gather that you have read the book?"

"Indeed I have," agreed Karstens. "It was published in 1550. People spoke a different kind of Dutch. Before that there was only a Latin text. And the Miracle of the Eucharist that could not be destroyed by fire is still remembered today. Every year we have the Silent Procession in Amsterdam." He grinned. "It's said that the prostitutes are extra busy at that time. More than a few men seem to sneak away from the procession."

DeKok rubbed his chin.

"You're well informed," he praised. "Especially in knowing the quotation. I presume it's accurate?"

Peter Karstens made a vague gesture.

"Of course it's accurate. By now I should know the entire text by heart and..." He paused suddenly and blushed. "You know perfectly well, DeKok, how I make a living."

The gray sleuth nodded resignedly.

"You fake old Dutch masters, French impressionists, Flemish miniatures... If it suits you, you create a fake." He snorted and rubbed his nose with a little finger. "For instance, an almost unique book about a miracle."

Peter leaned forward and placed his glass on the table.

"You have no proof."

DeKok shook his head.

"Proof is not what I want."

"Then what do you want?"

The inspector smiled.

"What do I want? Despite my unsalvageable bureaucratic soul, I want no legal proceedings against you. I simply couldn't charge you with anything. It would be useless. But for several days I've been occupied with an investigation regarding vanished women. The strange thing is that along with those women, a small book has also disappeared...a book about a miracle." He stopped and rubbed the back of his neck. "I know your reputation and I know the reputation of the man who handled the book. So I put two and two together and ask you what you know about that book."

Peter Karstens nodded to himself.

"I've indeed made a pair of copies."

It sounded reluctant.

DeKok showed his surprise.

"Two copies?"

 Peter Karstens shook his head.

"Three, actually." He leaned forward and groped underneath the settee. With a smack he placed two yellowed books in front of DeKok.

"She hasn't picked these up yet."

"Who?"

"That girl from Bad Bertus."

"Which girl?" demanded DeKok.

"Annie Scheepstra."

12

The next morning, cheerful and clean-shaven, DeKok entered the police station. A good night's sleep had done much to revive him.

At first he had trouble falling asleep. Four vanished women chained to fake miracle books spun around in his head like pieces of glass in a kaleidoscope. For a while he tried to make sense out of the whirling colors. But when that proved impossible, he forced the kaleidoscope out of his thoughts and finally fell asleep to the rhythm of his wife's delicate breathing.

As he passed the front desk, DeKok waved at Meindert Post, the Urker watch commander. But the large man had his eyes fixed on a computer screen and did not notice him. DeKok shrugged. Before computers came into his life, Meindert would never have been so absorbed as not to notice everything that went on around him.

In the detective room the gray sleuth found Vledder, too, peering at a computer screen. The world is being computerized, thought DeKok. How long before people are also loaded with chips and directed from some super keyboard? He kept the thoughts to himself.

The young inspector looked unhealthy, pale blue circles under his eyes. When he noticed his old partner he produced a wan smile.

"A few more nights like that and I'll be ready for a sanitarium."

DeKok looked worried.

"How late did it go last night?"

"I didn't get back to the station until almost two in the morning, and then I still wanted to enter as much as possible in the computer. I'm just reorganizing it now. Kusters said you had gone home."

DeKok nodded, remembering the previous night with fond memories.

"After a few glasses of a truly noble Burgundy, accompanied by a true artist and a tantalizing young woman, a man of my age longs for his bed."

Vledder looked suspicious.

"Where were you?"

"With Peter Karstens on North Market."

"The forger? I met him once. Doesn't he have a model who doesn't like to wear clothes?"

DeKok nodded slowly.

"Yes, Maria was there. But Peter is not just a forger, he's an artist," he corrected. "And Peter Karstens is certainly an artist when it comes to forgeries."

Vledder seemed at a loss.

"What did you want from him?"

"What does an upstanding police officer do when he visits a master forger?"

Vledder hesitated.

"Ask about a forgery?" He sounded unsure.

DeKok sat down behind his desk and leaned forward.

"I told you that in the past I have handled a few cases involving Bad Bertus. I have a pretty good idea of how he works. Whenever Bertus had an old painting or some other antique, he would immediately have a few copies made...forgeries he sold as the real thing."

Vledder's eyes widened.

"The miracle book," he whispered.

DeKok smiled.

"You get the idea?"

A bit of color returned to Vledder's face.

"And?" he asked curiously. "Did Peter Karstens make forgeries of the miracle book?"

DeKok nodded.

"He made three copies."

"Three?" asked Vledder, disbelief in his voice.

"Yes. One copy had already been picked up. There were two more copies waiting."

"For what?"

"For who...for Annie Scheepstra."

Vledder seemed stunned. Almost half a minute passed before he shook his head and came from behind his desk. He picked up a chair and sat down backward, his arms on the back of the chair.

"And I thought," he almost stuttered, "that you said, eh, that Bad Bertus had a relationship with Karstens?"

DeKok sighed deeply.

"That was the point from which I started. Believe me, I was just as surprised as you when Peter told me that the order for the forgeries came from Annie. Although

Peter referred to her as Bertus's girl, Annie handled the entire transaction herself. She negotiated a price by telephone and personally took the original miracle book to Karstens with an order for two forgeries. Later she picked up the original and one of the copies. The second copy was left behind so that Peter could make a third copy."

Vledder listened intently.

"And she never came to pick up the last two forgeries?"

DeKok shook his head.

"Peter still has them."

"Did you see them?"

"Yes, he put them on the table in front of me."

"Did you confiscate them?"

DeKok looked up.

"I left them there."

Vledder reacted with surprise.

"Why?"

The old inspector rubbed the back of his neck.

"The copying of such a book is not illegal," he lectured, "as long as you do not offer it for sale as real or original. And Peter has done no such thing."

Vledder threw his arms up.

"But those books could be of prime importance to our investigation."

"Peter Karstens will keep them safe, he promised me. And as soon as anybody shows any interest in the book, he'll let me know."

"And you trust him?"

"Absolutely."

Vledder snorted.

"I would have taken them."

DeKok ignored the remark. He sank back in his chair.

"There's something else," he said.

"What?"

"That miracle book, the original, isn't worth two million guilders—not even close. A hundred thousand would be a good price, if you can find someone crazy enough to go that high."

"Says who?"

DeKok spread his arms wide.

"Peter Karstens. He knows more about these things than anybody else you might name."

"And what does that mean?"

The gray sleuth did not answer. He stood up and walked over to the rack where he kept his coat. Vledder followed him.

"Where are you going?"

"To Purmerend."

"Again?"

"Yes."

"And what is it this time?"

DeKok stared at Vledder for moment. His face hardened.

"I'm going to ask Paul Voldrop why he expects Bad Bertus to come up with two million."

Vledder drove the old police VW through the Ij Tunnel at a reasonable speed.

"How many more times are we going to be driving to Purmerend?" he asked in a mocking tone. "We should request a trailer, then we can stay there day and night."

DeKok shrugged his shoulders.

"Maybe this will be the last time." He laughed. "Unless Dr. Aken suddenly cuts his vacation short."

"You expect that?"

DeKok shook his head.

"The doctor is probably going to remain absent for a while." He paused and glanced aside. "What happened in Amsterdam last night?"

Vledder sighed.

"I have it all in the computer. Why didn't you ask me at the station house?"

"Because I wanted to get going. Besides, I'm not interested in all the details right now. Just give me an overview."

"All right. Slotermeer Station has not followed accepted police procedures. They have been hasty, care-less, and incomplete. The names were not exactly right and not all the addresses were correct. It took a while to find the people."

"But you succeeded?"

The young inspector nodded. He took his notebook from an inside pocket and handed it to DeKok. The gray sleuth placed it on the dashboard, unopened.

"Just tell me. I have enough trouble reading your notes when I'm sitting at a desk. In the car it's just impossible."

"The disappearance of Marie Antoinette Houten," began Vledder, "was reported by her boyfriend, Karel

Bensdorf. They have lived together for more than two years. The disappearance of Charlotte Sloot was reported by her father."

"Were they referred to the hospital by their primary-care physicians?"

The young man shook his head.

"No referral. They both received a phone call. A simple phone call to come to Slotervaart Hospital…for a blood test."

"And?"

"They never came back."

"Did somebody take them to the hospital, as in the case of Rosie and Annie?"

"No. Karel had to work and Charlotte's father was needed at his business. Both women took a streetcar. They had been told the test would take less than half an hour."

"Were they called on the phone by a man or a woman?"

"I don't know. Actually, it never occurred to me to ask that."

DeKok pensively chewed his lower lip.

"Did you find out why the blood test was necessary?"

Vledder nodded.

"Apparently it was in connection with athletics. Both young women were active in sports. That's why they never questioned the call. They thought a blood test was nothing exceptional. They had participated in other tests, primarily in regard to the heart and lungs."

DeKok nodded his understanding.

"Did Karel and/or Charlotte's father check with the hospital?"

"Yes," said Vledder. "They were told that they had never heard the names before and that the hospital had never made a call for a blood test. They do not do that by telephone, only by letter."

DeKok rubbed his nose with a little finger.

"That was more or less to be expected," he said simply.

Vledder hit the steering wheel with a fist.

"And yet I don't believe it," he said sharply. "I bet that—"

DeKok raised his hands as if warding off evil.

"Any other similarities?" he asked calmly.

"No, no, there wasn't anything else. You have the gist of it."

"Were they ill?"

"Not really. There were some vague complaints… fatigue, and they coughed a little."

DeKok turned in his seat.

"And the skin of the face, had that changed? Was it tight?"

Vledder stared at the road. The color drained from his face. He was pale again.

"Charlotte's father," he said softly, "didn't know for sure…had paid no attention. But Karel Bensdorf noticed that his girlfriend's face had become tight with a strange, almost unnatural expression."

DeKok nodded with closed eyes.

Vledder turned into the parking lot. Again he drove to the other end of the lot and parked the car under the same bushes as before. They exited the car and walked slowly to the entrance of the apartment building.

The young inspector pointed at the façade of the building.

"We should have visited Paul Voldrop last time, when we were here anyway. We knew he lived in the same building."

DeKok's look contained a hint of censure.

"We had not talked to Bad Bertus for the second time, and we didn't know that Voldrop demanded a cool two million for a book that has a value of no more than five percent of that price."

Vledder made a nonchalant gesture.

"Paul Voldrop is an athlete, somebody primarily concerned with his own physical well-being. What does he know of antiques? Perhaps he just guessed that it was worth at least two million."

DeKok shook his head.

"That doesn't fit the facts. When Annie went to see Peter Karstens, he told her right away that she could expect at most a hundred thousand. And as far as we know, Annie and Paul are two hands on the same stomach." He laughed suddenly. "Whatever that means."

Vledder stood still.

"And in the meantime I understand less and less. Which miracle book did Bertus get from Annie? I don't think that the old pimp would have accepted a forgery."

DeKok nodded in admiration.

"That's a very good observation," he praised. "Bad Bertus knows quite a bit about antiques. I've been able to see that for myself, the few times I've had contact with him. I think that, although Annie ordered two forgeries, she showed the original to Bertus with the request to find a buyer."

Vledder walked on.

"Then," he said, "we have to assume that Annie disappeared with the original and at least one forgery."

DeKok nodded.

"Correct. I bet that Paul Voldrop knows all about Peter Karstens, the forgery, and the expected price. That's why I'm so curious as to why he demanded two million from Bertus."

"Perhaps," opined Vledder, "Voldrop knows a lot more about Annie's disappearance than he told us."

DeKok glanced aside and laughed.

"You're on a roll, aren't you? One theory after another."

Vledder shook his head and remained silent.

They entered the building. DeKok walked over to the panel and pushed the button for P. Voldrop and waited. There was no answer.

When an old lady entered the lobby from the corridor with the elevators, DeKok lifted his hat politely and took hold of the heavy door to keep it open for her. With Vledder in his wake he walked toward the bank of elevators.

"You know where we're going?"

DeKok nodded.

"The eighth floor, almost directly above Rosalind's apartment."

"You think they have rented it already?"

DeKok shrugged.

"Why don't you have another little talk with the super? Perhaps he has discovered some more about that strange removal."

Vledder nodded, pulled out his notebook, and made a note.

"Okay, boss."

DeKok gave him a hard look but did not say anything about the fact that he hated to be called "boss." It sounded too foreign to him. Not at all Dutch.

Meanwhile the elevator had reached the eighth floor and they walked down the corridor to Voldrop's apartment. They pushed the doorbell and waited. DeKok leaned on the bell a second time, creating a long and penetrating sound. Finally he let up and took a step back.

He looked up and down the corridor and then produced a small brass instrument from his pocket.

Vledder shook his head in disapproval.

"We can't just enter this flat. That's illegal. We lack the authority." He sounded worried. "We've had a lot of trouble with that before."

DeKok ignored him. He took a good look at the lock and then adjusted some settings on the little instrument. He inserted it into the keyhole and after little bit of wiggling, the lock clicked open.

It took less than ten seconds. He slowly pushed open the door. Loud music came from the interior. Carefully DeKok walked through the hall toward the sitting room, the sound growing louder. At the end of the hall, a door stood ajar. With the tip of his shoe he opened the door farther. Shocked, he stopped in the doorway.

Lying prone behind a low table was a well-built young man with a short neck. Over his shoulder hung the wide part of a red necktie. DeKok came closer and looked down at the man. The material of the tie was deeply embedded in the flesh of the neck. The inspector looked at the swollen face and recognized Paul Voldrop.

Vledder caught his breath.

"Dead?"

"Yes, strangled."

13

_____

DeKok looked carefully at the swollen face. In his long career he had seen his share of dead people who had been strangled. He was used to the circumstances. Slowly he straightened up. His knees creaked in protest.

He stepped across the corpse and let his gaze roam around the room. Without effort he saw and retained everything that passed before him. It was almost as if his eyes were the lenses of a movie camera—long years of training had strengthened this inherent ability. He was also looking for things that didn't fit.

The room looked cold and stark; the interior was primarily black and white. He was surprised that Paul Voldrop, who dressed in such vibrant colors, preferred this cool and impersonal decor. His gaze returned to the corpse.

"You notice anything?"

Vledder looked at the corpse.

"You mean the ends of the necktie?"

"Yes."

"They're on his back."

"And what does that mean?"

"That the killer was behind him."

DeKok nodded agreement.

"Correct. Paul Voldrop was approached from behind and strangled."

"With his own necktie?"

DeKok shook his head.

"I don't think so. Paul Voldrop is not the sort of man to wear conventional neckties. But, to be on the safe side, check his wardrobe."

Vledder turned on his heels, looking for the bedroom.

DeKok took another look around. He tried to imagine the situation at the time of the killing. Tried to reenact the moment that preceded the act of murder. There was no sign of breaking and entering on the door into the apartment. Therefore, it was likely that Voldrop let the killer in. There were no signs in the room of a struggle or a fight. Everything seemed to indicate that Voldrop was not afraid of the killer, did not suspect him—or her—of any murderous intent. He had turned his back on the assailant. That confidence, mused DeKok, had cost him his life. He thoughtfully chewed his lower lip. But where did the killer find the necktie? Had he brought the tie for that purpose, or had the red necktie formed part of his clothing?

Vledder returned.

"He doesn't seem to own a single necktie. His clothes are rather colorful, though. I found the jacket with the big yellow squares that he wore when he came to see us."

Thoughtfully Vledder looked at the corpse. "There's something strange about all this. Paul Voldrop is, eh, was an athletic guy...an amateur boxer. I mean, the killer must have been rather strong, otherwise there would have been signs of a struggle, at the very least."

DeKok smiled.

"Very good. I was thinking the same myself."

Vledder looked at his partner and spread both arms wide.

"But what do we do next?"

DeKok feigned misunderstanding.

"What do you mean?"

Vledder grimaced.

"We can't investigate this case."

DeKok rubbed his nose with a little finger.

"No," he admitted. "It's not our bailiwick. We'll have to notify the Purmerend police."

Vledder grinned.

"And how do we explain our presence in this apartment? We can hardly admit that we gained illegal entry with the help of an instrument invented by an ex-burglar."

DeKok laughed carelessly.

"We simply close the door behind us, descend in the elevator with appropriately somber faces, and present ourselves at the office of the building superintendent."

"Then what?"

DeKok grinned.

"We tell him politely that we have come to see Paul Voldrop, resident of this apartment, but that he has not reacted to our ringing. We have, however, reason to believe that he's at home, because we heard music. Therefore, if the super happens to have a master key or a spare key or, even better, if he will be so good as to inform the local police…" He grimaced. "You see, then we can be properly surprised when our colleagues make the gruesome discovery."

Vledder shook his head in disapproval.

"Sometimes I'm flabbergasted."

"Why?"

"That you weren't fired long ago."

"Ah, my boy, but you see, I solve almost all my cases."

The Amsterdam inspectors drove back to their hometown. Vledder, as usual behind the wheel, was thinking deep thoughts. DeKok lolled in the passenger seat, outwardly appearing to have not a care in the world. But behind the relaxed features of his face, his brain churned at top speed. The case, he found, was taking more and more serious turns. Until Paul Voldrop's death, there had been no murder in the case. That is, there were no corpses, and there were only guesses as to what happened to the missing women. There had been no fact of violence until the death of the young boxer.

He wondered what could have been the cause of this sudden turn of events...how he should fit the murder into the rest of the picture, or whether it fit at all. Was there a connection between the vanished women and the murder? Or was it a coincidence? Or was just Annie Scheepstra connected to the murder? And how did she fit into the big picture?

The gray sleuth examined his own feelings. In his long career he had learned to isolate himself from grisly, brutal, and violent death by building a wall around his inner being that allowed him to view the seedier aspects of his profession with objective detachment. It was a self-defense mechanism. But it had never succeeded in making him insensitive or heartless. Under it all he retained his innate compassion and sympathy for the victims. What set this case apart in his mind was the absence of feeling for Paul Voldrop. It left him cold to think that his emotions were blunted to the point that he had stopped caring about a victim. He decided to discuss it later with his wife. He had to smile—a romantic talk about bureaucratic insensitivity. Slowly and with some effort he pushed himself into a more upright position.

"Did you ask about the necktie?"

Vledder nodded.

"The Purmerend inspectors promised to take good care of the evidence. You may have it after the autopsy. They want to make sure that Voldrop's death was the result of strangulation and if so, that the necktie was used."

DeKok nodded his understanding.

"There's no hurry."

Vledder glanced aside.

"What do you want with it?"

DeKok scratched the back of his neck.

"I once solved a murder because of a necktie." He smirked. "Some tricks can be repeated."

"I remember that," said Vledder.

"I thought you would. It was also a reddish tie."

"Yes and—"

DeKok interrupted.

"Never mind. We can swap war stories some other time. What about the super? Did he have anything new to add?"

Vledder shook his head.

"Rosalind's apartment is still empty. Nobody has taken particular notice. He thinks the owners of the building have advertised an opening, but he wasn't sure."

"Oh, well, our Purmerend colleagues can sort that out. I must say that they acted very professional. Good cops."

Vledder grunted.

"You could have been a bit more explicit about the case's background, as far as we know it."

DeKok shook his head.

"Not yet."

"Why not?"

DeKok looked out the windshield.

"I don't want to awaken sleeping dogs at Slotervaart Hospital...not yet."

Vledder got the hint.

"I couldn't do anything about that," he apologized. "It's because—"

DeKok interrupted again.

"But I have been thinking about your observation."

"What observation?"

"That the killer must have been very strong."

Vledder gave him a pensive look. Suddenly his face lit up. One hand felt the deep scratch on his forehead.

"Richard Netherwood."

Vledder parked the car behind the station house. DeKok moaned softly as he hoisted himself out of the car. While Vledder locked the doors, the old sleuth ambled toward the front of the station as he tried to stretch the stiffness out of his bones. At the corner of Old Bridge Alley, Vledder overtook him.

"Did you notice?"

"What?"

"Buitendam was standing in front of his window. He must have seen us."

DeKok grinned.

"Then there's only one way out for us—flight, immediate flight to Little Lowee's place!"

Snickering like schoolboys, they took a shortcut to Front Fort Canal and from there to Old Acquaintance Alley. As usual, it was busy in the Red Light District. A dozen different languages could be heard around them, and the prostitutes did a land-office business. Vledder waved around.

"The city is crammed to the rafters with tourists."

DeKok nodded agreement.

"Tomorrow is the start of Sail Amsterdam," he said somberly. "I would have liked to have participated this time. But the end of our case isn't even in sight."

"That's too bad," said Vledder. "I know you were looking forward to seeing the ships."

DeKok shrugged at the inevitable. At the corner of Barn Alley he entered Lowee's bar. Vledder followed close behind.

They walked past the tables to the end of the bar and hoisted themselves onto bar stools.

Little Lowee wiped his hands on his apron and came forward. His friendly, mousy face gleamed with pleasure.

"Glad to see ya," he chirped.

DeKok pointed at the almost empty room.

"It's quiet here. No business, no tourists from Sail?"

Lowee shook his head.

"I ain't no fan of all that hullabaloo. I stick wiv' me regulars."

"Like us?"

The small barkeeper winked.

"Same recipe?"

Without waiting for an answer, he dove underneath the bar and emerged with their usual special bottle of cognac. With a quick, practiced movement he grabbed three snifters, placed them on the bar, and carefully poured generous measures. Then he picked up one of the glasses and raised it in the air in the direction of the inspectors.

"To all the kids of thirsty fathers."

DeKok grinned. He rocked the glass slowly in the hollow of his hand. He took a discerning sip. The warm glow of the liquid drove the last bit of stiffness from his bones. He replaced the glass on the bar after another, larger sip. He leaned toward Lowee.

"You know Blond Mina?"

Lowee looked pensive.

"Tha's one of them broads offa Bad Bertus?"

DeKok nodded.

"I would like to talk to her quietly, without anybody being the wiser. If I visit her, it will be all over the quarter in no time." He gave Lowee a penetrating look. "And I want to avoid that, you see?"

Little Lowee rubbed his face.

"You wanna 'er come to da station?"

"In about an hour, if possible." He laughed. "By that time the commissaris should be home."

Lowee laughed.

"So, itsa like dat again, is it?"

DeKok ignored the question.

"Can you take care of that?"

The barkeeper became serious.

"I's gonna make sure," he said with conviction. "She's gonna be there." He paused and cocked his head. "Blond Mina were sorta thick wiv' da gone broad, da Annie Scheepstra. Them broads was always together."

DeKok took a swallow.

"You're well informed."

Little Lowee grinned.

"Youse still gotta case?"

"Yes."

"And?"

"It isn't going too well."

Lowee thumbed in the direction of the window.

"Da guy of da broad came and done a lotta ruckus inda quarter."

"The boxer?"

"Yep."

"Where?"

"In front o' Bad Bertus. He were yellin' that Bertus knowed more about it."

"Annie's disappearance?"

"Exactum."

"Then what?"

"Bertus done come outside widda pistol and done tole' 'im to get off or he were gonna shoot 'im. He done left fast-like."

DeKok gave Little Lowee a sharp look. He watched for a gleam in the eyes, the slightest movement of a muscle.

"That guy," he said, "is dead."

The barkeeper put his glass on the bar. His hand trembled.

"Dead?" he repeated tonelessly.

DeKok nodded.

"Killed in his apartment."

14

DeKok had tired feet. The pain crawled from his toes across his insteps and past his ankles to his calves. It seemed as if a thousand tiny devils went to work on his legs with their small pitchforks. It saddened him; he knew what the pain meant. Although he had been assured, time and time again, that it was purely psychosomatic, the pain meant that the case he was working on was going badly. Whenever he had the uneasy feeling that he was drifting further and further from a solution, the little devils made their appearance and tormented him to the point of exhaustion.

With a pained expression, he lifted both legs and placed them carefully on the edge of his desk. A small sigh of relief escaped him as the pain abated slightly. Vledder looked worried. He was familiar with his partner's affliction.

"Tired feet?" he asked.

DeKok did not answer. He pulled up his pant legs and squeezed his calves gently between thumb and forefinger. Sometimes it helped.

"I thought Little Lowee's reaction a bit strange," he said pensively. "He didn't say it, but I got the impression that Lowee knows exactly who's responsible for Voldrop's death."

Vledder grinned.

"That doesn't seem all that difficult," he said conde-scendingly. "It's an easy conclusion to make."

DeKok looked up.

"Do you know who helped Voldrop into the next world?" he asked scathingly.

The young inspector waved a hand.

"Bad Bertus. It's almost elementary." Resting on both elbows he leaned forward and stretched out an index finger toward his partner. "Paul Voldrop threatened him...made a ruckus on the canal, accused him in no uncertain terms of the murder of Annie Scheepstra and, on top of it all, he demanded two million guilders." He grinned. "I'd think that would be motives aplenty for Bad Bertus."

The gray sleuth was irritated, and not just because of the pain in his legs. He shook his head.

"It's just too pat, too convenient," he said, irritated. "I don't believe in murder *en plein publique*. I've never encountered that. Murder is usually a matter of a small committee—a small, closed group of interested parties." He pushed down his pant legs and took his feet off the desk. The will to fight had returned to his eyes. "You're right, Bad Bertus as the killer is conspicuous because of its obviousness. But why?" He grinned briefly. "Because of facts that he himself reported? He came here to tell us that Paul Voldrop was threatening him. He said that the young man accused him of murder, and he said that Vol-drop demanded two million guilders." He shook his head. "You see, that's almost a confession of intent. He gave us advance warning that if Voldrop were to be murdered, he, Bertus, would have all the motives you could ask for.

And just that makes me suspicious of directing all our attention to that old pimp." He leaned forward and slapped his calves. "I think that's causing my tired feet."

Vledder smiled, but his face remained serious.

"If I understand you correctly," he said thoughtfully, "then Bertus deliberately put himself under suspicion by drawing our attention to him?"

DeKok nodded.

"That's what could be concluded," he said slowly. "But there are a few remarkable facets to the conclusion."

"Such as?"

DeKok rubbed his nose with a little finger. Then he studied the finger for a few seconds, as if he was seeing it for the first time.

"Just think," he said after a while, "Bad Bertus drew attention to himself before the murder was committed and that means—"

"That Bad Bertus," interrupted Vledder, "knew that Voldrop was going to be killed in the near future. And the question that elicits is—"

He was interrupted by a loud knocking on the door. It flew open to reveal a young blond woman. Her short black dress exposed long, slender legs ending in shoes with stiletto heels. The deeply scalloped décolleté showcased two perfect breasts. Over this revealing outfit she wore a large, beige raincoat, apparently borrowed in order to leave her place behind the window.

DeKok knew her by sight but had never met her personally. With a wide smile on his lips he walked toward her.

"Hello, Mientje," he said instinctively, using the childish diminutive of her name. Mina was short for Wilhelmina. "I'm happy you were able to stop by."

She looked up at him.

"Little Lowee sent me."

DeKok steered her to the chair next to his desk.

"Sit down," he said gently. He looked at her face. "You've been crying."

Vledder made some entries on his computer while keeping his eyes on the woman. He could hardly believe that this vision of loveliness was a prostitute, available to anyone for a price.

Blond Mina nodded and took a handkerchief from the sleeve of her dress.

"Lowee also told me," she said, "that they killed Fashion Paul."

DeKok sat down across from her.

"Is that what he was called, Fashion Paul?"

The woman nodded.

"Because he always wore the craziest fashions. But he was a nice guy. I liked him, and Annie was besotted with him. She often told me that if she had met Paul a few years earlier, she would never have been in the life."

DeKok pushed out his lower lip.

"High praise for Paul indeed."

"Sure. And he was serious about Annie. Sincere, I mean. They had plans for a wedding."

"And Bertus knew that?"

Blond Mina shrugged her shoulders. Her breasts threatened to pop out of her dress. Vledder held his breath, but the moment passed.

"I think so," answered Mina.

DeKok leaned forward.

"One evening you told Paul to come here and ask for me?"

"Yes."

"Why?"

Mina sighed deeply.

"When Annie disappeared and they told him at the hospital that she had never been there, he thought that Bad Bertus had ordered her killed. You see, that's what he wanted to prove."

"How?"

"By beating him long and hard enough until he confessed."

DeKok smiled discreetly.

"A method we're not allowed to use."

Mina seemed not to hear the remark. She worried nervously with the hem of her short dress.

"I didn't want for Paul to get into trouble. That's why I advised him to come here and ask for you. I thought that would be safer. You know how to handle such things."

"Did he listen to you?"

She shook her head.

"At first he wanted nothing to do with the police. I had to talk myself red in the face to convince him. I was glad when I did. Paul can't handle Bertus."

"What do you mean by that?"

She moved in her chair.

"That boy was no match for Bertus. Bertus has lived his entire life in the quarter. He knows where the bodies are buried, and there is little he has not experienced." She paused and her eyes filled with tears. "And you've seen it for yourself...Paul is dead."

DeKok held his head to one side.

"And Bertus was involved?"

She suddenly became animated.

"Of course he was involved." She stretched a hand out toward the inspector. "But if you can ever prove it, you're even more of a miracle worker than they say you are."

DeKok gave her a searching look. The sincerity of the young woman confused him.

"Why did Paul think that Bertus had Annie killed?"

She pursed her lips attractively, unaware of the effect.

"It's because Annie knew too much," she said finally.

DeKok narrowed his eyes.

"About what?"

Mina's face became red. To his surprise, Vledder suddenly realized she wasn't wearing any makeup.

"About everything," said the woman, "about everything that Bertus did."

DeKok looked puzzled.

"How, eh," he asked cautiously, "how could Annie know too much about his business? Bertus always plays it very close to the vest...no partners...a man who works alone...always. He simply doesn't allow prying eyes around him."

Mina allowed the raincoat to slip from her shoulders and gave a wan smile.

"Perhaps that was true in the past, but lately he did very little himself. Annie dealt with almost everything. She was on the road for him...negotiated his deals."

"Such as?"

She smiled again, but this time there was a hint of derision in her smile.

"Surely you don't think that I want to be found dead too one of these days?"

DeKok rubbed his face with a flat hand, a gesture designed to gain some time. He realized that he had few arguments that could convince the young woman to reveal the dark practices of the old pimp.

He looked at her with a friendly smile.

"Annie was your friend?"

"Yes, you could say that."

"She took you into her confidence?"

"Sometimes."

DeKok pulled out his lower lip and let it plop back several times. He stopped when he saw a look of disgust on the lovely face across from him.

"Why, eh, why," he asked, momentarily distracted, "I mean, why did Bertus allow Annie to take care of his business?"

"I think, it's because he's ill…sick."

DeKok was genuinely surprised.

"Sick?"

The young woman nodded.

"You can't tell to look at him; he looks healthy enough. But I think he's simply afraid to get out. He no longer drives his own car. It doesn't leave the garage. If he has to go somewhere, he takes a taxi."

"Did Annie ever mention it?"

"His illness?"

"Yes."

Blond Mina shook her head.

"No, never. It's actually my own idea. He shows himself so little lately. I noticed it."

DeKok stood up. He did not want to question her any further; he wanted to avoid having her say things she would rather not say. He put a fatherly arm around her shoulder.

"Go back," he said, "before they miss you."

The woman smiled.

"My time is my own. But if anybody gets curious, I'll just say I went out to lunch."

The gray sleuth picked up her raincoat and draped it around her shoulders.

"If there's something you want to tell me, stop by or give me a call."

She nodded and traipsed out of the room in her high heels. DeKok watched her leave. Behind him, the telephone on his desk rang.

Vledder leaned over and picked it up just as DeKok turned around. He noticed the young man's face turn pale.

"What is it?" he asked.

Vledder replaced the receiver.

"The watch commander."

DeKok looked at him expectantly.

"Well?"

"Richard Netherwood...he has taken a woman hostage."

15

"What kind of woman?"

Vledder gestured apologetically.

"The watch commander didn't know. The reports are still vague. He did send a few constables to Old Church Square. It seems that Richard suddenly attacked a woman on the dam near the national monument. He grabbed her from behind and held a knife against her throat. Dragging her through Bourse Street and Paternoster Alley, he forced her into the Old Church tower."

DeKok looked confused for a moment.

"Into the tower?"

Vledder nodded.

"Usually it's closed at this time of day. But today the door was open because of a guided tour. They had just left when Richard entered the tower with his hostage."

DeKok continued to be confused.

"Where did the report come from? Who reported it?"

"It seems that someone saw what happened and followed them from a distance."

DeKok shook his head. There was a grin of disbelief and confusion on his face.

"How," he demanded, "did that someone know it was Richard Netherwood?"

"He seems to have called that out, himself."

"Richard?"

"Yes."

With quick steps, DeKok walked over to the peg and grabbed his coat and his hat. He waved toward Vledder.

"Come," he urged, "before there is an accident."

Three steps at a time, they stormed down the stairs. Downstairs, DeKok approached Jan Kusters.

"Any additional news?" he asked.

Kusters nodded.

"He has that woman on the first rampart and threatened to throw her down into the square if the police tried to enter the tower."

DeKok looked worried.

"I hope they didn't do that."

"No."

"What does he want?"

Kusters shrugged.

"Who knows? The guy is nuts."

DeKok ignored the remark.

"You have a megaphone?"

The watch commander opened a cupboard and produced one. It looked new and unused.

"Careful with it. You're supposed to use the one in your car."

DeKok gave him an indignant look. With the megaphone in his hand and Vledder close behind, he left the station house.

There were large crowds on Old Church Square, their faces a mix of worry and amusement. With open

mouths and craned necks they stared up at the tower.
A young constable saw DeKok and approached.

"The tower guide," he explained, "had just finished
a special tour of the tower and church...some Germans,
in connection with Sail Amsterdam. That guy must
have seen the open door when he came from Wide
Church Alley."

"He went straight for the door?"

The constable shook his head.

"According to a witness who followed him from the
dam, he first went onto Warmoes Street, but then he
changed his mind and dragged the woman through the
alley to the tower."

DeKok nodded his understanding. He looked up and
could clearly see the figure of Richard Netherwood. He
held the woman with her back pressed against the rampart. The knife could not be seen from the distance. The
inspector raised the megaphone in front of his face.

"Richard," he called, "this is Inspector DeKok. I'm
coming up to talk to you."

Vledder nudged him.

"Let me do it. It is a bit of a climb to the first gallery."
He smiled gently. "You're not that young anymore."

DeKok pressed his lips together. Although he knew it
was the truth, the words of his young friend hurt. Reso-
lutely he shook his head.

"You stay here," he decided. "I'm going to see if I can
talk the endangered woman out of his hands. Make sure
she doesn't disappear too." Again he raised the megaphone.
"I'm coming up, Richard, and I'll listen to you."

There was no answer.

With a strange, queasy feeling in his stomach, DeKok approached the open door of the tower. Silently the crowd parted to let him through. As he reached the open door, he slowed. The tension was almost unbearable. At any moment he expected the body of a woman to smack into the bricks on the square.

He was very much aware of the risks he ran. If Richard executed his threat, the woman would be dead and he would be blamed for her death. He knew the fickle bureaucracy of the police department very well…his tenuous position as an inspector…the media, always in search of a scapegoat.

He took a few steps back and aimed the megaphone up at the sky.

"Richard," he called out, "don't do anything dumb. It won't help anybody…or your Rosie."

When there was still no answer from above, he sighed deeply, took a final look at the silent faces of the crowd, and entered the dark portal of the tower.

During the first fifty steps he maintained a good pace. Then his rhythm slowed gradually. His legs grew tired and his heart made loud protests in his chest. Young Vledder, he thought bitterly, had been right. His condition was not up to this type of exercise.

To regain his breath more or less, he stopped for a while. Then he discovered he was still carrying the megaphone. For just a moment he contemplated leaving it on the steps, but then his bureaucratic soul cried, City property! With a sigh, he resumed his climb.

It was cold and windy on the outside balcony of the tower. The wind whirled around with a deafening noise.

Amsterdam, from this height, he thought, almost seems like a miniature city. As far as the eye could see were small roofs, balconies, and narrow streets. Suddenly, as he followed the wall around, he saw Richard's back. Apparently the young man had not noticed his arrival.

For a moment DeKok contemplated a sudden attack, but soon thought better of it. Richard Netherwood, Vledder had told him, was a strong man and obviously quite unpredictable. Besides, a wrestling match in the confined space of the balcony seemed a bit risky.

Suddenly the young woman noticed his presence. Her brown eyes opened wide with fright. She opened her mouth, perhaps to speak, maybe to scream. Quickly DeKok brought a finger in front of his lips in the universal sign of silence.

High up the tower of the Old Church it seemed to DeKok that time stood still. The woman stared at him as if he were a specter.

For a moment the old inspector was at a loss, weak with indecision. It seemed as if his knees were ready to collapse at any moment. Slowly he lowered his back against the wall of the tower and sat down. The megaphone rested in his lap.

Suddenly Richard tensed and turned around, an expression of astonishment and bewilderment on his pale face.

DeKok looked up at him, spread his arms in a defenseless gesture, and smiled.

It was as if the sight of an exhausted old man aroused a feeling of pity in Richard and broke his resistance. A shy, almost childlike expression crossed his face. Hesitantly, with a shaking arm, he pointed at the woman.

"That's her."

His words were almost lost in the wind.

DeKok remained seated.

"Who?" he yelled.

Richard Netherwood pointed again and in a sudden lull of the wind his voice was clear.

"She...she took Rosie away."

DeKok leaned back in his chair and looked at her from across his desk.

"Who are you?"

She placed her hands in her lap and looked at him. Tears glistened in her brown eyes.

"Josie...Josephine Harkema."

"Are you injured?"

Her right hand touched her neck.

"No. I did feel the tip of the knife from time to time, but he didn't penetrate the skin." She stretched out her left arm and bent it a few times. "This is still a bit sore. He twisted my arm behind me when he picked me up."

"Dam Square?"

She nodded.

"Almost in front of the Beehive Department Store. I needed some things."

"Did you know the young man?"

Josephine did not answer.

DeKok leaned closer.

"Did you know him?" he asked, more insistent.

She nodded vaguely.

"By sight."

"Where did you meet him?"

"In, eh, in Slotervaart Hospital."

"You work there?"

"Yes, I'm a registered nurse."

The gray sleuth nodded his understanding.

"And in your capacity as nurse, you came into contact with the young man?"

"Yes."

DeKok held up an arm, an index finger pointing at the ceiling.

"That young man accompanied a young woman, his girlfriend Rosalind Evertsoord. She had received a referral to your hospital from Dr. Aken in Purmerend. She checked in at the counter in the lobby." DeKok became silent. He leaned back in his chair. "Then you, Josephine Harkema, came and took her away."

The nurse did not react.

DeKok tried to suppress his irritation, but his friendly expression quickly evaporated.

"You took her away," he said curtly. "Where did you take her?"

Josephine Harkema lowered her head. Tears streamed down her face and into her lap.

"I'm not allowed to say," she sobbed.

"Who says so?"

She looked at him with a teary face and shook her head.

"Nobody is supposed to know. Not yet."

DeKok pushed his chair closer. The hard features of his face softened. With a fatherly gesture he put a hand on her shoulder.

"You've been ordered to remain silent?" he asked.

"Yes."

"And you were ordered not to show yourself during the investigation at the hospital?"

Josephine nodded, her head down.

"They sent me home…a paid day off."

The gray sleuth gave her a measured look.

"The management of the hospital sent you home with pay?"

Again she shook her head.

"I can't tell you…I can't tell you…I can't tell you."

She repeated it over and over.

Slowly DeKok rose from behind his desk. Over the years he had developed an ability to sense the moment when it was time to stop an interrogation, when further questions became useless. This was the moment.

He looked down at Vledder.

"What have you done with Richard?"

The young man pointed a thumb over his shoulder.

"Same interrogation room as before."

Pensively DeKok chewed his lower lip. Then he seemed to have come to a decision.

"Send him home and tell him that he has to be here at Warmoes Street at exactly eight thirty in the morning."

Vledder's mouth fell open with incredulity.

"Send him home?" he repeated, still in shock. "He robbed this woman of her freedom…took her hostage."

"I know, I was there," DeKok said curtly.

Still stunned, Vledder pointed at Josephine Harkema.

"And…and…" he said, stumbling over his own words. "What happens to her?"

"Tell the watch commander to put her in a cell."

Vledder swallowed.

"In a cell? Are you crazy? Whatever for?"

DeKok looked at him without any emotion.

"As an accomplice to murder."

16

When DeKok entered the detective room of Warmoes Street Station unusually early that morning, he found Vledder busy at his computer. DeKok knew what he was doing: he had put all the information they had gathered into special files and was now piecing bits and pieces together to come up with several reports, each one a model of clarity and truth, but none reflecting the entire picture as they knew it. It was Vledder's own unique contribution to the partnership with his old mentor. At the drop of a hat, Vledder could produce a report that would satisfy the commissaris—or anyone else—without interfering with DeKok's ongoing investigation. It was an enviable skill.

DeKok approached and watched Vledder's fingers fly over the keyboard. The screen was changing faster than the eyes could follow. Noticing DeKok's shadow, the young man looked up with a worried look on his face.

"I was afraid you'd be late. I just got a series of reports ready that will keep them off our backs for a while."

"Why?"

Vledder pointed to a folded newspaper.

"The newspapers are filled with reports about the hostage situation in the tower of Old Church. Luckily there are no photos. But you can bet your life that when the commissaris gets here, all hell will break loose." He shook his head. "That's no good, you know. The commissaris shouldn't have to learn about cases in his own district from the newspapers. That's why I quickly concocted a report."

DeKok smiled.

"In your usual uninformative way, I hope?"

Vledder nodded.

"Just the facts, which he could read in the newspaper, and the names of those involved."

DeKok looked at the clock on the wall. It was a quarter past eight.

"If Richard Netherwood is on time, then we'll be gone before the commissaris gets here. For once I appreciate him keeping strict banker's hours."

Vledder shut down his computer after having printed out a report.

"Where are we going?" he asked.

"Slotervaart Hospital."

"With Richard?"

DeKok nodded emphatically.

"And with Josephine Harkema. That's the reason I had her locked up last night." He laughed gaily. "I understood why you thought I was crazy. And I don't really believe she is an active accomplice to murder. But it's an accusation I can legally defend." The gray sleuth spread both hands. "I had no choice. If I had released her, she would have immediately contacted the people who, for whatever reason, ordered her to remain silent. I wanted to prevent such an incident."

Vledder snorted.

"And that's why you incarcerated an innocent woman?"

It sounded like an accusation.

DeKok made an apologetic gesture.

"I did ask the watch commander to give her a good bed and to provide her with some comforts." His face darkened. "But it's not my fault she spent the night in the cells."

"Whose fault is it then?"

DeKok walked away, turned, and pointed a finger at his partner.

"You'll find out."

Richard Netherwood entered the detective room without knocking. He looked bad. There was no color in his face and his eyes had dark circles beneath them. He approached the inspectors.

"Did you, eh, did you speak with her? The nurse, I mean."

"Yes."

"And is…is Rosie dead?"

DeKok looked grave.

"Together," he said with determination, "we're going to find out the answer to that question."

DeKok was the last one to struggle out of the car. The old VW was not built to accommodate four people. He and Josephine had crawled in the backseat, while Richard had taken the seat next to Vledder. He stretched and looked up at the building. Ponderous and massive, like an

ugly monster of steel and cement, the Slotervaart Hospital
rose into the air. A strange anxiety came over him...an
inexplicable fear as he peered up at the rows of windows
reflecting the bright sunlight like so many dead, glassed-
over eyes.

Richard Netherwood stood next to him. It was as if
the young man guessed his inner turmoil.

"A terrible building, don't you think so?"

DeKok nodded vaguely.

"A gateway," he murmured.

Richard glanced at him from the side.

"To life...or to death?"

DeKok took a deep breath.

"Both."

Vledder and Josephine Harkema preceded them across
the parking lot. DeKok and Richard lagged about ten
yards behind. As they approached the main entrance of
the hospital, DeKok increased his pace and closed the gap.
The inspector was aware of the possibility that the nurse,
once in familiar surroundings, would find a way to disappear into the bowels of the building.

Nobody took any notice as she led the three men
to the elevator. They got off on the seventh floor then
walked through a roomy hall and a set of double doors as
she led them to a wide corridor.

DeKok kept a sharp eye on the nurse and detected an
increasing nervousness in her step and movements. Half-
way down the corridor she stopped and pointed to a door
to the right.

"There, you need to go in there," she said with a
broken sob and walked away.

With a captivating smile, the gray sleuth took her by the arm.

"We do not want to lose the pleasure of your company."

Gently but decisively he led her to the door she had pointed out.

"Perhaps you can announce us?"

He turned the doorknob and pushed her through the open door.

A graying man sat behind a large desk covered with files and folders. He did not appear surprised to see them. Looking amused, he folded his newspaper and placed it on the desk. Slowly he rose from his chair and smiled.

"I'm afraid," he said calmly, "that our game is over."

DeKok took a step closer.

"You're Dr. Bemmel?"

The graying man nodded.

"Chief surgeon and director of this hospital." He gave the man in front of him a measured look. "And you're Inspector DeKok?"

The old inspector bowed slightly with old-world charm.

"With, eh, a kay-oh-kay...at your service."

Dr. Bemmel pointed to the newspaper on his desk.

"I had expected your arrival, more or less. Although the newspaper reports said that the names of those involved were not known, I realized that the entire hostage situation had something to do with what happened here in the hospital." He pointed in the direction of Josephine Harkema. "May she leave? She isn't guilty of anything. She just did what we told her to do."

DeKok tilted his head to one side.

"We?"

The director waved vaguely in the direction of an empty chair next to his desk.

"Dr. Lesterhuis and I."

"And he's not available?"

Bemmel shook his head.

"Dr. Lesterhuis will arrive late in the afternoon. He rescheduled a number of appointments from this morning until later because he had to take care of some private matters."

The director-physician again pointed in the direction of Josephine. "May she leave?" he asked with more emphasis. "I don't think anything is served by having her stay."

DeKok nodded slowly to himself. After a while he turned to the nurse.

"I'm sorry for all the troubles and discomforts I've caused you," he said tiredly. "I sincerely hope you will not hold it against me. I hope you have no feelings of resentment." He sighed. "I promise, I will explain later why I don't deserve your resentment."

Josephine Harkema gave him a wan smile, turned around, and walked out of the room.

Dr. Bemmel sighed.

"I have a great deal of admiration for Josie. It wasn't easy for her. But from the start she kept her word."

DeKok pointed a thumb at Richard Netherwood.

"Until his violent kidnapping forced her to capitulate. She must have died a thousand deaths on that tower."

Bemmel's face fell.

"If anyone is to blame, it's me." He nodded in DeKok's direction. "I'm sure that you're curious how four young women could so mysteriously disappear in my hospital." He remained silent for a few minutes. Then he seemed to shake himself. "But mysterious it isn't," he continued. "We created the mystery ourselves."

"How?"

Bemmel brought strong, slender surgeon's hands together, pressing his fingertips.

"In hindsight, the answer is so simple...as the result of an unreasonable panic, a number of foolish decisions were made...decisions that left the door open to suspicion."

"Such as?"

The doctor grimaced. Slowly he looked up at DeKok.

"Don't you know?"

DeKok felt himself getting angry with the slow pace of the conversation. He was on the verge of giving in to the berserker rage that sometimes plagued the usually placid and complacent Dutch. He lifted his chin and gave Bemmel a searching look.

"I will hear about your stupid decisions in due time," he said with exasperation in his voice. "I want to know where those women are and what happened to them. And I want to know now!"

The doctor remained silent. A shaking hand reached for a set of folders on his desk.

Vledder looked worried. He knew that DeKok was near the end of his patience and stood ready to intervene.

With a determined look on his face, DeKok walked closer to the desk and rested both hands on the edge.

He leaned forward menacingly. A nervous tic began in the corner of the doctor's eyes.

"Where are they?!" he almost roared.

Again, Bemmel did not answer at once. He looked past DeKok and gazed at Richard Netherwood. Then he lowered his head.

"In a small cemetery," he whispered. "A small cemetery in Ermelo."

17

_____

Richard Netherwood cried soundlessly. Tears dripped down his cheeks and disappeared into his collar. His body shook. DeKok placed a comforting arm around his shoulder. The young man swallowed.

"Rosie is dead," he uttered. "I knew it all along. Rosie is dead." He shook his head. "But why didn't they tell me that?" He wiped the tears of his face with the back of his hand. "They could have told me, they should have told me. They…"

DeKok led him to a chair and made him sit down. Then he returned his attention to Bemmel.

"All four?"

"What do you mean?"

DeKok exploded. Vledder tensed.

"That's the last time you answer one of my questions with a question," roared DeKok. "I'm sick and tired of your cat-and-mouse game. You answer my questions now and in full, or I'll arrest you on the spot for kidnapping and murder. I've had it with you, you understand?"

The doctor paled. He grabbed a number of folders and hastened to answer DeKok.

"Yes, all four women are buried there: Rosalind Evertsoord, Annie Scheepstra, Charlotte Sloot, and

Marie Antoinette Houten." He pushed the folders away. "Before I became director here, I had a similar function in a psychiatric hospital in Ermelo. From that time I knew about the cemetery there. In the old days, before my time, patients who died in the institution were sometimes buried there. It seemed a good place. Private and very shady."

"But why?" roared DeKok. The doctor moved back in his chair, obviously afraid.

"It, eh, it was the publicity. There would have been too much publicity if we had used a regular cemetery here in town."

Vledder placed a firm hand on his partner's arm, sensing that DeKok was on the verge of jumping across the desk and strangling the doctor.

"What was the problem?" asked Vledder.

The doctor looked relieved at the young man's interruption.

"Ebola," he said.

"What is Ebola?"

"A terrible disease. Almost always fatal. After infection, there is no way out. And it is fast—sometimes it takes a few days and sometimes only a few hours. The disease looks similar to the plague, the Black Death from the Middle Ages. But even more contagious. Especially in the final phase, when the lungs are infected. Then even the saliva that the afflicted bring up when they cough contains enough particles of the virus to infect someone standing nearby."

DeKok threw up his arms angrily.

"And the women who disappeared had that disease?"

Bemmel nodded.

"It is to Dr. Aken's credit that he immediately recognized the symptoms in Ms. Evertsoord. Not only that, he deduced that this was a new, more virulent strain. He had just read an article by Dr. Lesterhuis that speculated that new and more virulent strains were likely."

DeKok had calmed down a little. He shook off Vledder's hand with a grateful look at his partner.

"That's why he contacted Dr. Lesterhuis here at the hospital?"

"Exactly. Dr. Lesterhuis is considered the expert on the subject in our country. He immediately grasped the seriousness of the situation and came to see me."

"Then what?"

Bemmel stroked his head with both hands. It was a tired and defeated gesture.

"As I told you, in our panic we did a number of foolish things. But you should understand our fear...we were very much aware of the social responsibilities. The spread of the Ebola virus is so epidemic that the consequences cannot be calculated. Thousands have died within weeks of an outbreak, especially in Africa, where it originates. There is no cure, but the virus can be contained by denying it new hosts. We were afraid of a panic, especially in a city that is filled beyond capacity due to Sail Amsterdam."

DeKok chewed his lower lip.

"So you decided to keep all of this a secret?"

Bemmel sighed.

"In our panic we went too far, committing almost criminal acts. But we had no idea what to do in the event of such a calamity and were obsessed with the idea that no one should find out…all traces of the carriers of this terrible disease had to be erased." He paused and glanced with a worried look at Richard Netherwood. "Ms. Evertsoord died within hours of when she came in. We were afraid that you, too, had been infected. But your blood tested negative. It may be a small consolation to you, but Ms. Evertsoord did not suffer."

Richard had recovered slightly.

"But how did that disease get here? How did Rosie get infected?"

Bemmel lowered his head slightly.

"There, too, we have made mistakes. We did not give the question of the origin enough thought. Our first objective was to tend to Ms. Evertsoord, do whatever we could. Only after her death did we wonder who else, besides Mr. Netherwood, could have been infected and where the infection originated. In her handbag we found a membership card from a basketball organization and a photo of her and two other women. There was a note on the back of the photograph giving the names of the women and the place where the photo was taken: Tanzania. Ms. Evertsoord toured with the basketball team through Central Africa, playing exhibition games. We were almost sure that the women had been infected there."

Vledder rubbed his chin.

"Do you expect more cases?"

Bemmel shook his head.

"Not from the same source. They would have been evident by now. The incubation period is short."

The old inspector pointed at the folders on the desk.

"I'll take those with me," he announced.

"Of course," said Bemmel.

"You'll get them back, eventually."

"Yes," said Bemmel resignedly. "But I urge you not to make anything from the files public…not for the time being." He smiled sourly. "Otherwise everything has been for nothing."

DeKok looked at him.

"I'll keep it quiet, for now. But sooner or later it will be brought to light how you have tried to play God, and it may mean the end of your career. There have been criminal actions. At the very least you have denied the friends and relatives of these women to part with them peacefully. I will let you know what actions are to be taken regarding the secret funerals outside the jurisdiction of Amsterdam."

"Of course," sighed Bemmel.

"By the way," said DeKok suddenly, "are you familiar with the Miracle…the Miracle of Amsterdam?"

Bemmel looked puzzled.

"What kind of miracle?"

DeKok smiled.

"I can hardly tell you," smiled DeKok, "how happy your answer makes me."

They were back at the station. Vledder put the folders next to his computer with a feeling of accomplishment.

"All hell can break loose now," he declared with satisfaction.

DeKok smiled.

"You mean the hell the commissaris, in the form of the devil, is likely to raise?"

Vledder nodded with emphasis.

"He doesn't have a leg to stand on. Neither does the judge-advocate. Here it is...in black and white...the results of our investigations; that is, the evidence that our investigation of the vanished women had a legitimate basis. It also explains the behavior of Richard Netherwood, the kidnapping of Josephine Harkema, and the ruckus in the hospital after that staged screening." He raised both arms in a gesture of triumph. "And all the complaints about our behavior have evaporated as a fog in the sun. We can dismiss them and throw them in the trash. The circular file, as they say."

DeKok gave him a quizzical look.

"There are no more questions?"

Vledder was visibly annoyed.

"What kind of questions?" he asked with a hint of uneasiness in his voice. "Rosalind's car in the canal? The work of Bemmel's driver. The sudden departure of Dr. Aken? At Bemmel's request. The emptying of the apartment in Purmerend? On orders of Bemmel." He paused and gave DeKok an admiring look. "That smell...you were right. Her apartment had been disinfected."

The old man snorted.

"I may not be able to climb a tower without some difficulty, but my nose is still in excellent shape. I keep it that way by sniffing cognac whenever I have the chance."

Vledder powered up his computer.

"I'll concoct a supplementary report that will blow the commissaris away...complete with the testimony of Dr. Bemmel and his actions, orders, and requests." He grinned boyishly. "With an extra copy for our colleagues in Slotermeer Station and a copy for the secretary of health, education, and welfare."

DeKok leaned closer.

"So there are no more questions?" he repeated.

The young man made some preliminary entries on his keyboard. He looked up with annoyance.

"Why are you pushing on about questions?"

DeKok leaned back.

"I'll mention a name: Annie Scheepstra."

Vledder shrugged.

"What about Annie Scheepstra?" He patted the stack of folders with a flat hand. "She died of a new, rather virulent strain of Ebola. It's written down in full detail by an expert in the field and countersigned by the director of Slotervaart Hospital."

DeKok sighed deeply.

"Did she play basketball?"

"What has that to do with anything?"

"Everything. Rosalind, Charlotte, and Marie Antoinette belonged to a Dutch ladies' basketball team that made a tour in Central Africa. Annie Scheepstra was not there. You see, she could not have become infected in Africa."

Vledder reacted angrily.

"She lived in the same apartment building as Rosalind Evertsoord. Perhaps the women knew each other...they met in the elevator, for instance. And that's how Annie became infected."

DeKok grinned.

"Richard Netherwood," he declared calmly, "who maintained a more or less intimate relationship with Rosalind, was not infected by her. That's a matter of record. And do you seriously maintain that a hypothetical encounter in an elevator caused an infection?"

It sounded cynical.

"It's possible."

DeKok passed a hand over his gray hair.

"Sure," he said tiredly, "it's possible. Everything is possible. But that doesn't make it realistic." He paused for a moment and took a deep breath. "And then there is something else...the faces of Rosalind, Marie Antoinette, and possibly that of Charlotte had a peculiar expression because of the disease. An expression that Richard called 'the mask of death.' As far as we know, Annie Scheepstra did not have that mask."

Vledder pushed his keyboard aside.

"She had the same symptoms," he said with emphasis. "The same symptoms as Rosalind...otherwise, Dr. Aken would not have referred her to Dr. Lesterhuis."

DeKok nodded agreement.

"She said that she had those symptoms, and it's possible that just on the basis of her own complaint Dr. Aken referred her to Slotervaart Hospital." He stuck out his chin and hit the edge of his desk with a fist. "But did Annie Scheepstra really have those symptoms? Was she really tired and listless? What did her athletic boyfriend tell us? He said he had trouble keeping up with her." The gray sleuth shook his head with conviction. "Annie Scheepstra does not fit in with the other three women."

Vledder grimaced as he pointed at the stack of files.

"Is that wrong?" he demanded angrily. "Are these lies? Is that extensive description of the diagnosis completely incorrect?"

DeKok did not answer. He stood up from behind his desk and started to pace up and down the room slowly, in his typical waddling gait. Somewhere, he mused, there had to be a solution, a plausible explanation for a folder full of contradictions. While he subconsciously avoided the obstacles in the room he searched feverishly for a solution.

Jan Kusters entered the room and interrupted DeKok's pacing with an outstretched hand. He gave him an envelope.

"That's been delivered for you."

"How?"

"By a boy."

"What kind of boy?"

Kusters gestured with irritation.

"Who knows? Suddenly it was on the desk with your name on it and a kid of about ten years slipped out of the station."

"You could not catch him?"

The watch commander seemed close to an apoplexy.

"No!" he roared. "And what's more, I didn't even try."

DeKok nodded to himself, and Kusters, visibly upset, left the room.

The old inspector tore open the envelope and pulled out a note.

Dear DeKok,

Enclosed is an invitation for an extensive tour of the harbor aboard the Neptune, *a beautiful, comfortable flat-bottom. The boat will visit all participants in Sail Amsterdam.*

Yours,
 Lowee

P.S. Bad Bertus purchased a plane ticket for New York.

The note was written in an educated script and without a single misspelling. No one would have guessed that Lowee, who almost always spoke his own peculiar thieves' language, was capable of producing such an elegant little note.

Vledder came closer and read the note by looking over DeKok's shoulder.

"A clear hint," he concluded.

DeKok nodded.

"A hint from Lowee and a heads-up for quick action," he grinned. "I suspect that Lowee had our weak extradition policies in mind."

"You think he knows more?" asked Vledder.

DeKok shook his head.

"In that case, Lowee would have come himself."

"So what do we do?"

DeKok replaced the note in the envelope and studied the invitation. It was made of expensive paper. At the top was a picture of the *Neptune*, and the text was engraved in elaborate scrollwork.

"A beautiful boat."

Vledder nudged him.

"What do we do?" he repeated.

DeKok turned around.

"Do you remember what Mina said about Bad Bertus?"

Vledder nodded.

"Yes. If you can ever prove something against him, you're even more of a miracle worker than they say you are."

"Exactly."

"So we don't do anything?"

DeKok did not answer. Pensively he looked into the distance. A few feet away, the telephone on his desk rang. Vledder automatically turned around and picked up the receiver.

"It's for you," said Vledder after listening to the caller.

DeKok accepted the instrument resignedly. He did not like telephones.

For several minutes he listened attentively. Then he said, "Thanks, Peter," and hung up.

Vledder looked at him expectantly.

"Who was that?"

"Peter Karstens."

"What did he say?"

For moment it looked as if DeKok had withdrawn into himself. Unapproachable, lost in thought. His gaze was still vague when he looked up.

"Take Fred Prins and Appie Keizer with you, if they're available. Otherwise get some uniforms."

"Where am I going?"

"Slotervaart Hospital."

"And then what?"

"Arrest Dr. Lesterhuis."

Vledder's mouth fell open.

"Dr. Lesterhuis?"

DeKok nodded.

"For murder."

18

They were seated in the cozy living room in DeKok's house. All tension had disappeared and they stretched out on comfortable reclining chairs. The gray sleuth lifted a bottle and pointed at the label.

Vledder laughed.

"I can't read it from here, but I'm sure it's a rare bottle. By all means, pour it."

DeKok nodded.

"A small present from Little Lowee. He had it delivered this morning."

Mrs. DeKok entered the room from the kitchen. She carried several platters of delicacies. Vledder hastened to help her while DeKok poured.

"It's pure bribery," said Mrs. DeKok, looking at the bottle. "That's the only name for it. Just like that elegant invitation to attend Sail Amsterdam."

DeKok shook his head.

"I can't be bribed." He grinned boyishly. "Nobody can afford to pay my price. Lowee must have made a misstep somewhere, and that caused sorrow in his sinful heart...thus the cognac. The invitation I received earlier."

Vledder nodded agreement.

"When you sent us to Slotervaart Hospital to arrest Dr. Lesterhuis," he paused thoughtfully, "how did Lowee make a mistake? What misstep?"

DeKok raised both hands.

"First, the cognac."

Young Vledder laughed and watched as his partner warmed some large snifters over the blue-yellow flame. He thought about how many times he had been in this room...in an easy chair, cognac in one hand and delicacies within easy reach, while he listened to how DeKok had tied the loose ends together and brought the case to a close. With barely concealed admiration, he looked at the slightly flattened nose, the deep grooves around the mouth, and the coarse gray hair.

"Little Lowee," he remarked, "has again proved his worth. He drew our attention to the disappearance of Annie Scheepstra."

DeKok passed glasses all around and looked at Fred Prins. He liked the quiet detective; he was the type of colleague who was always ready to help out, to assist whenever he was asked, without a lot of questions.

"Is Appie Keizer running late?"

Fred Prins shook his head.

"Appie has been assigned to a pickpocket detail and couldn't get away."

Vledder suddenly leaned forward and made a sneezing noise that sounded suspiciously like a short, sudden burst of laughter. The cognac almost escaped his glass.

"You were going to tell us how Little Lowee made a misstep," he said hastily, recovering his composure.

DeKok smiled at the impatience of his younger colleague. They both knew that Vledder had a tendency to jump to conclusions without either enough facts or enough thought.

"Little Lowee," he said calmly, "was convinced that Bad Bertus was responsible for the death of Paul Voldrop."

"And that wasn't so?"

"Not directly. I mean, the idea for the murder did not originate with him."

"Who, then?"

DeKok took a swallow from his glass and calmly, with eyes closed, savored the amber liquid. Vledder was about to urge him on when DeKok continued.

"Before it becomes a bit confusing, Prins, too, wants to understand what happened, and he wasn't there all the time. Therefore it seems polite to make certain things as clear as possible." He placed his glass on a small table and leaned back in his chair. "Annie Scheepstra," he explained, "was not at all a dumb, quixotic little girl, as Bad Bertus wanted us to believe. On the contrary, she was highly intelligent, attuned to her environment, and a quick learner."

"What is—" began Vledder impatiently.

DeKok held up a hand to silence him.

"Bad Bertus," continued the old man, "is not just a pimp with about a half a dozen attractive girls in a well-run brothel, but he's also a less-respectable dealer in art, antiques, *and* cocaine. In my own defense, I have to say that I was not certain that he was a drug dealer, although I suspected it from time to time. At the time that I actively investigated him, before I was permanently assigned to homicide, the drug trade was not yet the problem it is today. It was a side business, and most of the underworld wasn't interested."

"Hard to believe, nowadays," remarked Fred Prins.

"Yes, I suppose it's progress. But to get back to the point, because of his dealings in art and antiques and such items, Bad Bertus had a lot of contacts among what we call 'the better situated.' When the desire for cocaine became fashionable among the affluent, Bad Bertus was one of the first to fill that need. And Bertus was very smart."

DeKok took a sip and savored it.

"One of his oldest contacts," he continued, "was Dr. Lesterhuis, a physician of international renown. Lesterhuis owns a large estate in the country, and under the expert leadership of Bertus, it soon became a center for the distribution of cocaine."

Vledder laughed bitterly.

"I'm still at a loss. Where does Annie Scheepstra fit in? And what about the other women?"

DeKok ignored the interruption.

"At first," he continued calmly, methodically, "Bad Bertus took care of the delivery himself. He personally took the stuff to Lesterhuis, who had meanwhile become an addict, for further distribution to his rich friends. That is, until a young prostitute applied to Bertus's brothel. She caught his attention."

"Annie Scheepstra."

"Right. Bertus, who usually avoided women, was captivated by the young, eager prostitute. He discovered qualities in her, a competence that went beyond being just a prostitute. So one day, when he was unable to make a delivery in person, he sent Annie. As I said, Annie was a quick learner. She soon had a very good idea of the kind of business Bertus was involved in. She also picked up some useful information about his dealings with art and antiques...Bertus was in the habit of having a number of copies made of any valuable piece he laid his hands on. He had a number of forgers on his payroll, so to speak."

Vledder grinned.

"Peter Karstens."

DeKok nodded.

"Peter was one of them. He was usually called upon in the case of a painting, or printed material. He had others on tap for furniture or metalwork, for instance."

"The miracle book," said Vledder.

"Yes, when Annie Scheepstra inherited a number of yellowed papers and the miracle book, she knew who to contact."

"Who's Peter Karstens?" asked Fred Prins.

"An artist...and an expert forger," answered Vledder.

DeKok sighed.

"When Peter Karstens told me the story behind the miracle book, I realized for the first time that Annie was more—much more—than just another prostitute. From pure laziness, Bertus had pushed more and more business her way...took her more and more into his confidence. You have to keep in mind that Bertus, too, was getting older. He needed help."

DeKok paused and lowered his head before he continued.

"Probably Bertus's lucrative business activities would have continued indefinitely under Annie's expert stewardship if Annie hadn't suddenly fallen in love with an ambitious amateur boxer."

"Paul Voldrop."

DeKok bit on his lower lip.

"And that was the beginning of the drama."

Mrs. DeKok looked at her husband.

"Love and drama, they're as closely related as love and happiness."

The gray sleuth nodded agreement.

"Annie Scheepstra had," he sighed, "known little of love in her short life, and happiness was a new feeling for her. That's why she clung to Paul with all the passion of which she was capable." He took a deep breath and drained his glass. "We will never know," he continued after a while, "if Paul exploited her love, her devotion. For Annie's sake let's hope that he meant well, as Blond Mina said, and was seriously committed to Annie. Therefore it's to be hoped that the original idea was hers."

Vledder moved to the edge of his chair.

"What idea?"

"Extortion."

The young inspector was taken aback.

"Extortion?"

DeKok nodded.

"Paul Voldrop wanted to build a sports complex. Therein he wanted to open a boxing school, and he hoped to give some direction to the disadvantaged youth of Purmerend. But that took money, a lot of money. Paul estimated at least a couple million. Annie took the plan to heart and became obsessed with it. She knew almost to the penny how much money Bertus had. But when she approached him and explained the plan, he laughed at her. He laughed even harder when Annie tried her hand at extortion. But Annie had other options. She had visited Dr. Lesterhuis several times on Bertus's business errands. And Lesterhuis did not laugh. He felt really threatened by Annie's blackmail and feared for his reputation as a physician. Lesterhuis contacted Bertus and demanded Annie's death. But the pimp wanted nothing to do with murder. He advised Lesterhuis to pay up or not, at his option. But he refused to consider murder. 'My reputation isn't worth a murder,' he said."

DeKok paused and poured another round.

"Then," he said hesitantly, "the Ebola virus entered the picture. Rosalind Evertsoord arrived at Slotervaart Hospital and died within hours. And that gave Lesterhuis an idea."

"He was going to infect Annie," said Vledder, shock and horror in his voice.

"Yes. He called Annie and told her he was prepared to pay her the two million guilders. He would give her the money if she came to the hospital. But, in order to alleviate any suspicion, it had to look as if Annie was just another patient. Lesterhuis told her what symptoms she had to fake when she went to see her own physician, Dr. Aken. Dr. Aken, so he assured her, would refer her to Slotervaart Hospital."

"And Dr. Aken was fooled?" asked Prins.

"Yes, Lesterhuis had prepped her well. Annie did exactly as Lesterhuis had told her. But she was careful. She asked Bertus to take her to the hospital. Bertus did just that, and on the way there Annie told him that Lesterhuis had agreed to pay. Strangely enough, Bertus believed it. He did not become suspicious until several hours later, when Annie did not return."

"She was already dead then?"

"Yes, Lesterhuis made a full confession. Only he hasn't told us how he killed Annie. It's most probable that he infected her and then made a report similar to the one for Rosalind. Dr. Bemmel countersigned it without question. But we don't know if that is what happened. Therefore the judge-advocate has ordered the exhumation of Annie's body."

Vledder cocked his head to one side.

"And what about Paul Voldrop...who killed him?"

DeKok gestured.

"Lesterhuis. Lesterhuis killed him. Although the scheme for the murder was all his idea, the impetus was provided by Bad Bertus. Bertus had a problem: he did not know how much Annie had told Paul. He thought it was a bit strange, to say the least, that Paul demanded a couple million from him and not from Lesterhuis. That made him suspect that Paul knew nothing about Lesterhuis. Because Paul's behavior annoyed him, he called Lesterhuis and told him that Paul, and not Annie, was the brain behind the extortion."

Vledder whistled softly.

"And Dr. Lesterhuis committed a second murder."

"Exactly."

The young inspector gripped his head with both hands.

"What a case," he moaned, "what a case." He paused, thinking. "But why did you order the arrest?" he asked suddenly. "I mean, how did you know Lesterhuis was guilty?"

DeKok smiled.

"First, I was convinced that Annie had not been infected with the Ebola virus when she went to the hospital. In my opinion she wasn't sick at all. And second, I knew that Annie had been in Slotervaart Hospital. I corrected an oversight of yours."

"My oversight?"

DeKok nodded.

"I had that cabdriver traced, the one who transported Bertus and Annie that morning. The driver knew Bertus very well. He had often had him in his car. He remembered him as a big tipper. And he remembered the woman who was with Bertus." He looked up. "Then there was the phone call from Karstens," he added.

Vledder narrowed his eyes.

"Did someone inquire about the book...the book about the miracle?"

DeKok shook his head.

"Peter Karstens made a small mark on all his forgeries so that he could always recognize his own work. Yesterday morning, Lesterhuis stopped by and asked him to make a copy of a book he had run across."

Vledder swallowed.

"Annie's book....the copy."

DeKok nodded.

"It was in her handbag, which Josephine Harkema had turned in to Lesterhuis with Annie's other personal belongings."

DeKok sighed deeply. The explanation had tired him.

He picked up his glass and drained it in one long swallow.

Mrs. DeKok looked at her husband.

"And Bad Bertus, he got off scot-free?"

Her husband shook his head.

"Members of the narcotics section arrested him at Schiphol when he tried to board a plane for New York."

Vledder raised a hand.

"This afternoon I received a call from the police in Purmerend. They wanted to know if you still need that necktie that was used to strangle Paul Voldrop."

DeKok shook his head.

"No longer needed."

"What did you want it for?"

The gray sleuth rubbed his nose with a little finger.

"That, my dear Dick," he smirked, "I'll tell you the next time we have a murder involving a necktie."

Mrs. DeKok left to make coffee and the conversation turned to lighter topics. Prins eventually said good night, soon followed by Vledder.

"I still have a lot of paperwork to clean up," he said as he shook hands with his old partner.

It was a nice summer evening with a balmy breeze and a gorgeous red sky. On the express advice of his wife, DeKok wore a light sweater under his sport jacket.

With a feeling of pure delight he got out of the taxi at the quay where the *Neptune* was moored. He stepped on deck and felt the traces of his seaman's blood invigorate him. DeKok was from an old and long line of sailors, the first to make his living on shore. If the island on which he was born had not become a hill in the now dry Zuyder

Zee, he might also have become a fisherman. He would never know.

At exactly eight o'clock the old skipper ordered the lines cast off and aimed the luxurious boat for the center of the Ij River.

Suddenly an old, ramshackle VW raced along the quay to where the boat had been moored and a young man, wildly waving his arms about, jumped out of the car.

DeKok recognized Vledder

The young man roared across the water.

"Another young woman has been killed!"

For a moment, DeKok hesitated. With longing he looked at the graceful ships along the river.

Then he formed a funnel with his hands.

"I can't understand you!" he roared back.

Vledder yelled again.

"Another young woman has been killed!"

DeKok shrugged and spread both arms in a gesture of defeat. With happiness he saw the distance between the boat and the shore steadily increase.

The skipper came to stand next to him.

"That young man yelled something."

DeKok nodded.

"I thought so, too, but sometimes I have the same complaint my mother used to have."

The skipper showed polite concern.

"And what is that?"

DeKok grinned.

"Sometimes I can't hear what I don't want to hear."

ABOUT THE AUTHOR

A. C. Baantjer is one of the most widely read authors in the Netherlands. A former detective inspector of the Amsterdam police, his fictional characters reflect the depth and personality of individuals encountered during his nearly forty-year career in law enforcement.

Baantjer was honored with the first-ever Master Prize of the Society of Dutch-Language Crime Writers. He has also been knighted by the Dutch monarchy for his lifetime achievements.

The sixty crime novels featuring Inspector DeKok written by Baantjer have achieved a large following among readers in the Netherlands. A television series based on these novels reaches an even wider Dutch audience. Over 100 episodes of the *Baantjer* series have aired on Dutch channel RTL4.

Known as the "Dutch Conan Doyle," Baantjer's following continues to grow and conquer new territory.

DeKok and the Dead Harlequin

This latest Baantjer mystery delves into a grotesque double murder in a well-known Amsterdam hotel. Inspector DeKok must unravel clues from a six-year-old girl who has trouble sleeping and a respected accountant who seeks DeKok's advice on committing the perfect crime.

DeKok and the Somber Nude

The gray sleuth is forced to deal with a most gruesome murder: a naked, dismembered young woman has been found in the city dump. DeKok faces death as an inevitable part of life, but when things turn this macabre, it's a hard pill to swallow.

DeKok and the Geese of Death

DeKok takes on a man accused of bludgeoning a wealthy couple. The killing urge is visibly present in the suspect during questioning, but did he commit this particular crime? The answer lies within a strange family, deadly geese, and a horrifying mansion.

DeKok and Murder by Melody

"Death is entitled to our respect," says Inspector DeKok, who finds himself once again amidst dark dealings. A triple murder in the Amsterdam Concert Gebouw has him unveiling the truth behind two dead ex-junkies and their housekeeper.

DeKok and the Death of a Clown

A high-stakes jewel theft and a dead clown blend into a single riddle for Inspector DeKok to solve. The connection of the crimes at first eludes him.

DeKok and Variations on Murder

During one of her nightly rounds, housekeeper Mrs. Van Hasbergen finds a company president dead in his boardroom. She rushes up to her apartment to call someone, but who? Deciding it better to return to the boardroom, she finds the dead man gone.

DeKok and Murder by Installment
Although at first it seemed to be a case for the narcotics division, this latest investigation soon evolves into a series of sinister murders involving drug smuggling and child prostitution.

DeKok and Murder on Blood Mountain
The trail of a recent crime leads Inspector DeKok to Bloedberg (Blood Mountain), Belgium, a neighborhood in Antwerp. Seems a man was fished from the Scheldt River, and DeKok has been summoned to help with the investigation.

DeKok and the Dead Lovers
Inspector DeKok and his partner Vledder are ordered to protect the art treasures of a millionaire. During their watch, they are called away to a murder scene where a victim has been handcuffed to a radiator and shot in the head. That same night a priceless ewer is stolen from the exhibition. The case is a most gruesome jigsaw puzzle.

DeKok and the Returning Corpse
Sandra Verloop has won a contest to meet a famous Dutchman. Her choice: Inspector DeKok of the renowned Warmoes Street Station. Sandra shows during a most disturbing case. DeKok and Vledder are on the hunt for a corpse.

DeKok and Murder in Bronze
Within the confines of the respected Ancient Guild of Bell Ringers medieval customs are practices on a regular basis. But when one of the members is killed under the Muider Gate, DeKok and Vledder must penetrate the public veil of the secretive guild.

For a complete catalog of our books, please contact us at:

speck press

4690 Table Mountain Drive, Suite 100
Golden, Colorado 80403
e: books@speckpress.com
t: 800-992-2908
f: 800-726-7112
w: speckpress.com

Our books are available through your local bookseller.